BELGIAN FLATS

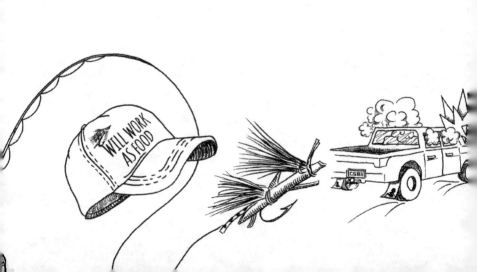

BELGIAN FLATS

CHRIS SANTELLA

LYONS
PRESS

Essex, Connecticut

An imprint of Globe Pequot, the trade division of
The Rowman & Littlefield Publishing Group, Inc.
4501 Forbes Blvd., Ste. 200
Lanham, MD 20706
www.rowman.com

Distributed by NATIONAL BOOK NETWORK

British Library Cataloguing in Publication Information available

Library of Congress Cataloging-in-Publication Data
Names: Santella, Chris, author.
Title: Belgian Flats / Chris Santella.
Description: Essex, Connecticut : Lyons Press, 2024.
Identifiers: LCCN 2024015155 (print) | LCCN 2024015156 (ebook) |
  ISBN 9781493085392 (paperback) | ISBN 9781493085408 (epub)
Subjects: LCGFT: Sports fiction. | Nature fiction. | Novels.
Classification: LCC PS3619.A5724 B45 2024 (print) | LCC PS3619.A5724 (ebook) |
  DDC 813/.6—dc23/eng/20240403
LC record available at https://lccn.loc.gov/2024015155
LC ebook record available at https://lccn.loc.gov/2024015156

♾️™ The paper used in this publication meets the minimum requirements of American
National Standard for Information Sciences—Permanence of Paper for Printed Library
Materials, ANSI/NISO Z39.48-1992.

This book is for my wife and best friend, Deidre, who's been ever so accommodating and gracious over thirty years of angling adventures. I also owe my daughters, Cassidy and Annabel, and our rescue Chihuahua, Lola, a special thanks for feeding my fishing passion. I hope they'll continue to visit the waters we've enjoyed together for years to come.

CONTENTS

Contents

CHAPTER ONE

F350s Pack a Punch

IT WAS WHEN A WOMAN I DIDN'T KNOW ASKED IF I'D LIKE TO snort some cocaine off of her breasts that I realized a change of scene might be in order.

The occasion was Halloween night, the unofficial end-of-season celebration for Belgian Flats' guide corps, a motley assemblage of trout bums, alcoholics, and assorted others who'd proven largely unable or unwilling to work at or hold down a more conventional job. There were roughly forty of us who limped into this little burg in the southwest corner of Wyoming each April or early May for the main fishing season . . . though if you owned a good pair of mittens, a propane heater and a sturdy constitution, you could find good fishing on the Blue year-round. Of the forty, twenty-five were die-hards, returning, against all odds, year after year; the rest were journeymen who kicked around: one year Alaska, one year Montana, maybe one year trying to toe the line with an uncle's contracting outfit or some other non-fishing nonsense.

It was difficult to say whether it was my personal appeal or the inspiring properties of the cocaine that had brought my new acquaintance to her current endeavor, though I imagine it was the latter. Cocaine can inspire unconventional behavior, I've observed, though I have never been an adherent of the powder myself.

Before any snorting or other sundry activities could be brought to fruition, the double-wide trailer where the festivities were proceeding bucked as if it had been struck by a freight train. My new friend fell backward, and the air erupted with a mix of curses and screams—the latter coming from the professional ladies who'd been recruited from over in Rock Springs, where they generally serviced the mining concerns—as everyone spilled out the front door. A locomotive hadn't derailed and careened south from the Union Pacific line, but the automotive equivalent—a Ford F350 XLT with a drift boat in tow, for good measure—rested against the southeast corner of the double-wide. It was the vehicle of one JD Smithers, the dean of the Blue's guide corps. After deflating his airbag with the Bowie knife he always kept strapped at his side, JD spilled out of the cab, falling face first in the mud. A few bottles and a haze of marijuana smoke followed him out. From somewhere in the mud, a voice bellowed, "Hope you saved me a lady, 'cus JD's pipes are a little backed up."

He certainly knew how to make an entrance.

No one was 100 percent clear how JD Smithers had landed in Belgian Flats. Some said he'd come south from the Henry's Fork after being caught with his waders down with the wife of a long-time client who happened to be a senior member of the George W. Bush administration. Others said he was running weed in Delacroix Parish east of New Orleans between redfishing clients, until the climate became a bit too hot for such endeavors. JD would allude to both versions of his past from time to time, though confirm nothing. But every May 1st since 1998 he would drive into Belgian Flats, usually in a brand-new Ford pickup towing a custom Clackacraft drift boat, rack up 150 guide days on the Blue, and drive out on November 1st. He was as vague about his winter itinerary as he was about his past. Most of us concluded that he headed south to a hideaway in Costa Rica or Patagonia, though for all we knew he could have holed up in Cincinnati and worked at a cousin's accounting firm.

JD's exact age and heritage were equally baffling. His ruddy skin hinted at Native American ancestry, but could just as well have been the cumulative effects of sun, wind, and alcohol. He might have been a dissipated thirty-eight or a dissipated—but well-preserved—sixty. JD was shaped like a refrigerator, but could move with surprising grace for a man his size when the situation called for it. (The evening in question was *not* one of those occasions.) There were four things we knew for sure about him:

1. He preferred Ford pickups.

2. He called every client (and most other guides) "Bud," probably because he couldn't or didn't care to remember anyone's name.

3. He liked Sierra Nevada Pale Ale and would have it shipped into Belgian Flats by the truckload, in cans, as the nearest liquor store was in Rock Springs and didn't always carry Sierra products.

4. If the fishing was slow or he was ever in doubt, he would tie on a size 10 purple Chubby Chernobyl and instruct sports to skate it in front of the boat.

As he struggled to right himself in the mud, someone called out "What's your costume, JD?" A second voice chimed in "Drunk!," another, "Fishing guide!"

"How about 'Horny Motherfucker?'" JD bellowed, finally standing and snatching a half-consumed beer out of the hand of the nearest reveler, who was dressed as a clown or a member of the Insane Clown Posse, it was hard to say. "We're done here," he added, stretching his arms to take in the truck, the trailer and perhaps the Blue River and the current fishing season. "Let's get this party started." JD thrust himself toward the door of the double-wide, his acolytes—which included basically everyone—laughing and following him inside. He eyed me as he passed. "Talk to me tomorrow, Cody. Rita's. At nine." The door closed. The squeals of the Rock Springs ladies—no doubt occasioned by JD's arrival—could be heard 100 yards away over the thumping bass of Iggy Pop's "Lust for Life" as I stumbled down the rutted road toward the trailer I shared with the Barnes brothers. I felt oddly proud that JD had remembered my name.

Chapter Two

Good Money for a Kid

What had led me to Belgian Flats, you might ask? Well—what leads anyone anywhere? The pursuit of a beloved (or at least someone you hoped might one day love you); an escape from a former beloved; an immature fantasy; a seeming opportunity; a favor to a friend; a change of scenery; and perhaps most of all, inertia. There are a handful of spots around the continental United States that can support a legion of fly-fishing guides through an extended season, generating enough bookings to make getting their lazy asses to said spot at least mildly worthwhile. These would include the Sacramento River in and around Redding California; the Henry's Fork west of Yellowstone in Idaho; the Madison above and below Ennis in southwestern Montana; and, of course, Belgian Flats and the Blue. (For those inclined to cast flies in saltwater, you could throw in Islamorada in the Florida Keys; Homosassa, north of Tampa; and the marshes east of New Orleans.) Like the inevitable arrival of blossoming flowers—or locusts—the guides would drift in. Paying clients—"sports," in the lexicon of another generation—flowed to these places thanks to their abundance of fish . . . or at least the lore concerning an abundance of fish. These days, every river seemed to be in decline. The joke used to be that if you wanted good fishing, you should've been here last week. Now it should be "last decade" . . . or "last century." But the sports still come.

Old ways die hard.

I came to guiding the way most guides get here—I liked to fish. I started plunking worms for bluegill with my uncle Bill on a pond in Baker City, Oregon, when I was five or six. Soon I graduated to casting Blue Fox spinners for trout in the Powder River, which ran through the center of town. By age ten I was on to fly fishing, and never looked back. No one mentored me; even in the worm days, Uncle Bill was far more interested in chatting up the young mothers that would wheel their charges around the park than my angling activities. I don't know what drew me to fly fishing. I hadn't ever seen anyone do it, and this was several years before *A River Runs through It* appeared at the Multiplex and ruined the pastime for at least a decade to come. Perhaps it was a sporting magazine I'd cracked open during a doctor or dentist's visit. A full-page spread showing the grace of the fly cast. The minimalism of the materials needed to create a fly certainly appealed. Whatever it was, I was (pardon the pun) hooked.

A year or so into my obsession, a neighbor passed along a battered mail-order catalog from Kauffman's Streamborn, a legendary fly-fishing store over in Portland. From that point on, all of my allowance and any nickels and dimes I made from odd jobs went toward fly-tying supplies—feathers, fur, hooks, etc. (My purchased materials were augmented with hair and feathers that could be harvested from roadkill; I wasn't proud!) By age fourteen, I wasn't a half bad tyer; sometimes I could sell my creations to old-timers I'd find at the fly-fishing-only section of the Powder below the Thief Valley Reservoir, fifty cents a fly. Maybe they thought it was cute that a kid was out hustling flies. But I think they saw me hooking fish and wanted in on the action.

When I was a freshman in high school, a conflict occurred that I've come to see as a seminal moment. I was a husky kid and tall for my age, and the football coach—an embittered former

Kansas City Chiefs linebacker who'd torn his ACL in his first regular season game, ending his career—saw a future for me on his line. (There weren't many kids in the high schools of eastern Oregon then, so linemen played offense and defense.) It was nice to be wanted, so I signed on. The coach insisted that we practice all summer long, mornings and evenings. I didn't have a problem with working hard, but I resented the evening practices—that was the time when the insects hatched and the trout fed on the surface. Before the official season started, I quit. One night I came back from my nightly river trip to find the coach sitting in my living room with my parents. He excused himself, though not before giving me a lingering look. I felt like a quarterback in the middle of a blitz.

Dad came to my room and explained the situation. "The coach says you'd make a good lineman," he said, "but that you've got some commitment issues."

"I guess that's true," I replied. "When it comes to football." I told dad about the evening practices and that that was the best time to fish. "If I have to choose between football and fishing, it's not much of a choice." He nodded.

"I'll call and let him know." As he was closing the door, he turned back. "You know, I always thought football was kind of a stupid game," he said.

I'll always thank him for that.

My parents insisted that I attend college, and I wasn't opposed to the idea. I'd always enjoyed reading. And it wasn't like I had any other plans. There was only one caveat—that the institution be within a reasonable distance of some first-rate trout fishing. Given my very average grades and the dearth of fishing-proximate schools, the short list we came up with was—well, short. At the top, there was the University of Montana in Missoula; Montana State University in Bozeman; and the University of Oregon in Eugene. Missoula and Eugene were almost equidistant from

Baker, and I liked the idea of getting out of Oregon for a while. Missoula got the nod.

U of M did not offer a major (or even a minor) in trout fishing, though if they had shown interest in such an addition to the university's offering, I had a curricula ready:

- Introduction to invertebrate insects
- The cast: forward, roll and spey
- Fly-tying I, II, and III
- Strike indicator or bobber: a moral question
- Essential elements for a summer fishing road trip
- Trout bums versus *Dharma Bums* (developed in collaboration with the comparative literature department)
- Whitefish: the other trout
- What fly anglers can learn from worm slingers
- Steelhead: are they trout or salmon?
- The great trout streams of northwestern Montana
- The great trout streams of southwestern Montana
- The great trout streams of _____ (region here)

You get the idea.

I declared English as my major—partly because of that fondness for reading, and partly because of a professor I met in English 101 (a core course), Jay Coachman. I don't know much about the habits of writers, but it seemed that Jay kept himself extremely busy. When he wasn't teaching, he cranked out books of poetry, novels, literary criticism, and book reviews for *USA Today*. Some of his poems seemed to touch on fishing:

Mayflies Are Out
Your short, fragile lives

8

Are a gift, a flagrant sacrifice
To those who seek you
For food
Or something more.

Professor Coachman owned an aging but indestructible Alumaweld drift boat and loved to fish, but he had a terrible time rowing; his boat rotated in circles from put-in to take-out as he tried to wrestle the oars into submission. When it came out during one class that I liked to fish, he recruited me as his oarsman. I'm not the best rower out there, but I can hold a boat in place while my fellow angler casts and can keep it off the ledges. These qualities endeared me to Professor Coachman. We had some fine days on the Big Blackfoot and the upper Bitterroot with that old aluminum tub. By my senior year, Professor Coachman was even able to float easier stretches with the bow aimed downstream, thanks to my tutelage. My schedule was heavily weighted toward classes that Coachman taught, a patchwork syllabus that zigged and zagged between *Beowulf* and Beckett, depending on his yearly whims. I wouldn't say that he inflated my grades, but he certainly cut me some slack, especially if an essay deadline dovetailed with a significant insect hatch.

I did my best to make Coachman's classes, but otherwise attended the bare minimum of scholastic sessions to get by, focusing my energies on Rock Creek, twenty-five miles or so east of campus. A budding trout fisherman could hardly hope for a better classroom. It's open year-round, varies greatly in character from its headwaters to where it dumps into the Clark's Fork and offers a boatload of hatches. It's also one of the few places where you'll find five different species of trout—cutthroat, rainbow, brown, bull, and brookie—depending where you fish. Plus, it's gorgeous. Rock Creek presented me with many gifts: my first moose sighting, my first brown trout over twenty inches, and my entrée into guiding.

Though in retrospect, the latter was perhaps less a gift than a curse.

Back in those days, there were a couple guides working Rock Creek. It was a pretty easy walk-and-wade gig, close to town, and the university crowd kept a steady flow of clients coming through, especially after "the movie" hit (my sophomore year). Everyone, it seemed, wanted to try fly fishing. (And every man wanted to look like Brad Pitt too, I'd guess.) One of the guides, Marty Schick, saw me out there so much he figured I was trying to cut in on his action. Marty certainly knew how to catch fish, but he wasn't big on social graces. He surprised me one day in the early spring as I was working the Skwala stone hatch. "Who you gonna be working for, then?" he called, with no effort at a greeting or other introduction. I was startled, but didn't want to let on.

"I'm not working for anyone," I replied, without turning around. "Right now, I'm fishing."

"You know what you're about, then?" A decent rainbow gulped my fly before I could respond, and I gently set. "I guess that answers my question. Wanna make some good money? At least for a kid?"

I started a month later and got a call whenever Marty had an overflow . . . which the summer after "the movie" came out, and the following summer too, was almost every day. "I don't know anything about guiding," I said to Marty a few days before my first engagement as we fished a little run below one of the campgrounds that fill up with U of M kids and their floaties on warm May weekends.

"You don't need to know anything. Just take 'em fishing. Tell 'em to cast where you'd cast. Tie on the bug you'd tie on. If they can't cast, show 'em. If they can't walk, hold 'em. They're payin', but you're the boss." Over the years, I came to realize that there were other nuances to being a competent guide . . . or at least a guide that a paying client would want to book a second time. That came later. Marty paid me $100 a day, plus tips, which *was* pretty good money for a college kid with no skills beyond a decent roll cast. Years later I realized he was charging my sports $350 for the privilege of sitting in my junker pickup and following me up and down the stream, pocketing $250 for himself.

I guess that's how you learn.

CHAPTER THREE

Das Kapital

JD WAS ALREADY SITTING AT A SIX-TOP TABLE IN THE CENTER OF Rita's when I arrived a few minutes before nine, though there were a number of two-toppers available. A few other guides were crowded around smaller tables they'd mashed together, apparently uninterested in incurring JD's wrath by suggesting he take a smaller setting. JD looked no worse for wear from what had no doubt been a long night at the double-wide, nor did he look particularly good. He was just JD, clad in his typical guide uniform—khaki nylon trousers with stains on both thighs, a faded blue 50 UPF fishing shirt with a hemostat clipped to one pocket, and a pair of polarized—and mirrored—sunglasses. He had a few different ball caps that he favored while fishing; the one he sported that morning advertised a now defunct fly-tying concern, with the likeness of a Muddler Minnow holding a sign that said "Will Work as Food."

"Cody," he said as way of greeting, tilting his head in the general direction of the five empty chairs around him. I weighed the unspoken messages my seat selection might send. Sitting at the end of the table would suggest I was usurping authority. Sitting opposite and one over would suggest asymmetry. Sitting next to him would just be weird. I sat across.

Rita's was an institution in Belgian Flats, if only because it was the only commercial establishment in Belgian Flats. In addition to being a restaurant, it served as a gas station, laundromat, and poorly provisioned general store—not an uncommon retail assemblage in the rural west, especially, it seemed, around fishing destinations. If they were to use a slogan, it might have been "A little bit of everything, none of it very good." Perhaps this was part of Rita's merchandising strategy; the guide corps that made up the bulk of her clientele was none too choosy. (Fortunately for visitors, there was a fly shop about five miles up the road, in Clemmons, the only business in *that* burg.) Just about every guide in Belgian Flats met their clients here, as there was parking and it was just a short walk to the put-in for Section One, the most popular float on the Blue. Most ordered breakfast. Since the crowds tended to materialize at the same time each day, Rita had streamlined the Early Bird menu to two items: the Blue River Plate, which featured scrambled eggs, a deep-fried hash brown patty, white toast and bacon; and the Veggie Head, which was the Blue River Plate, without the bacon. (Vegans were out of luck.) Rita, whose prim grannie dresses and overdone eye shadow made me think of a Victorian librarian who'd gone on a long bender and never quite returned, usually personed the tables. Her significant other, Roger, toiled in the kitchen, wearing a t-shirt that didn't appear to have been washed since the Carter presidency.

Rita came by our table and smiled at JD. He was one of her best customers during the season, and he usually got his clients to pay. As she asked for our order, her left eye twitched. I couldn't tell if it was a nervous tic or an attempt to flirt.

"Two Blues, Rita," JD said.

"I've got biscuits this morning," she replied, the tick increasing to the speed of a hummingbird's wings in hover mode. "Just for you and your . . . friend."

"That sounds lovely, Rita. Bring the toast too."

As Rita wheeled toward the kitchen, JD turned his attention to me.

"So Cody. What are you doing?"

"I was thinking I might do a quick float on the One this afternoon, if the cloud cover holds."

"With your life, Cody," he replied with the world weariness of Sisyphus as he watched his rock roll down the hill for the seven billionth time. "With your life."

Our plates arrived. JD's had a double serving, which Rita knew to bring without asking. "Just how you like it," she purred, with a few eye tics a la carte for good measure.

"I hadn't really thought much about it," I said, which was true. I had a regular client coming over from Seattle for three days of fishing the following day. After that, no plans. I figured I would head over to crash with my parents for a month or two and catch the tail end of the steelhead season on the John Day and Grande Ronde, maybe the Clearwater too. After the holidays, I thought I might load up my pickup and head to Mexico—either Baja, where I could chase roosterfish, or the Yucatan, where I could target bonefish and permit. The fee from my Seattle client alone could easily cover a month down south, two if I camped. And there were always plenty of collegiate *gringas* around looking for a little fun. Some were so drunk—or had such bad judgment—that even I could fit the companionship bill, at least for a few days.

"You're not dumb, Cody," JD said through a mouthful of eggs. "But right now your existence lacks what might be called a narrative arc. A purpose."

"A raison d'etre," I blurted out, hoping to impress JD with—what? One of my five French phrases?

"Yes, Cody. A raison d'etre." Though with his faintly Southern accent, it sounded more like someone who dated raisins. "I've seen a lot of boys like you come through here. And elsewhere." He leaned in and narrowed his eyes over the *elsewhere*. He wasn't going to reveal his winter haunt to me quite yet. "Here's what happens to most of them: For a while it's a good life. Even a great life. You work hard, but you play hard, too. You rub shoulders with some guys who've led some pretty interesting and even success-ful lives. You're not tied down anywhere. And you're fishing—or at least around it—all the time! You've got a lot of cash in your pocket, and if you're not a complete drunk or skirt-chaser, you've got a wad left at the end of the season that you'll probably drop on a new truck or something else that doesn't quite fill the little hole that's growing in your soul. That's the American way. In the offseason you screw off around a ski resort, or you do a little con-struction work with your high school buddy's cousin. Or maybe you head to Argentina or New Zealand or Belize and guide down there for a while. It's all pretty chill." JD paused to delicately but-ter his biscuit, half of which he daintily popped into his mouth.

"This goes on through your twenties, your thirties, on into your forties. Maybe you tie flies, and one of the big companies picks up a few of your patterns. Maybe you get an endorsement or two. That's another couple thousand in your pocket, and a closet full of gear that you don't really need. If you were thinking ahead, maybe you took that wad at the end of the season and picked up a thirty-year fixed for a double-wide or a little bungalow. If you're not too smart, maybe you also picked up a wife and a kid or two to fill up the house. But until your next day on the water, you've got pretty much nothing. When you hit your mid-forties, the problems start. Dropping your boat in one day, you make a funny turn and your back goes out. Or you take a cast in your eye the one moment you took off your sunglasses to scratch your nose. Or you total your new truck when a moose steps in front of you as you're heading back to Rita's to drop off your clients at the end of another day. And your insurance company drags their feet. Suddenly you're SOL. There's no money coming in, you probably don't have much saved, and you barely have the skills to work at Home Depot or McDonald's . . . if there's even a Home Depot or

McDonald's in driving distance. And that won't cut it anyway." He popped the other half of the biscuit into his mouth, sans butter.

"Are you familiar with the writings of Marx, Cody?" he continued, his voice somehow clear despite his cluttered mouth.

"The *Communist Manifesto*?" I ventured.

"That may be his best-*known* work. But I believe that his most important writing is contained in *Das Kapital*. The notions of exploitation of labor? Surplus value? The owner controlling and profiting from the means of production? Does any of this resonate with you?"

"Vaguely." I knew about supply and demand from the Intro to Economics class I'd taken my freshman year at U of M, but I was pretty sure that was something different.

"Perhaps if I were to give you some context, it will help." He placed the sugar dispenser in the center of the table, and the jam caddy and salt and pepper shakers at equidistant points around it. "In this model, the owner is Jack Hatch, and he's in the middle. The jam, salt, and pepper are workers—you, Jody, and Hal."

"But I don't work for Jack," I protested.

"Please listen for the sake of the model, Cody. Each time Jack books a trip, a client pays him $500. Jack then calls you, Jody, or Hal and offers you the opportunity to take his anglers fishing. He offers you $300. What happens to the other $200?"

"Jack snorts it up his nose." Jack was widely known to have a cocaine problem.

JD sighed, a sign that his patience might be waning. "We're not concerned so much with what Jack does with his proceeds, but the fact that he's exploited you as his laborer. He's taken $200 that should rightfully belong in your pocket. You're rowing the boat, after all. You're tying on the flies and netting the fish, aren't you? If Jack has booked you, Jody, and Hal, he's making twice as much coin as each of you. For picking up the phone. Does that seem right?"

I thought for a moment. "Well, Jack's made a little reputation for himself. He built up a clientele, and he takes the time to reach out to them. No one's forcing Jody or Hal to pick up the phone when Jack calls with a date. I guess I don't begrudge him the two bills." As an afterthought, I added, "I hear he provides lunches for guides *and* clients."

JD brought his fist down on the table hard, rattling my Blue River Special and upsetting my water glass, sending a small trickle toward the plate that held my as yet untouched biscuit.

"Dammit, Cody," he yelled. "I don't think you're getting the point. *You* need to be the *exploiter!*" The yelling turned all the heads in Rita's in our direction. Rita's eye was flickering like a teletype machine. JD looked in the direction of the guides at the huddled tables by the window, and their head snapped back down to their specials. "What I mean to say, Cody," he continued in a much softer voice. "You stay a guide all of your life, you're gonna wake up one day with no way to make a living, and not a pot to piss in. Maybe you can still go fishing. But there's more to life than fishing."

I needed to consider this, so I excused myself to visit the restroom.

Chapter Four

Be Careful What You Ask For

EVERY THIRD CLIENT I'D TAKE OUT WOULD OBSERVE—USUALLY after I'd netted a particularly large or difficult-to-fool trout—that he'd give up his office job in a second to work out on the water. "Look at your office!" they'd gush.

"Out fishing every day!"

"Get to know where the big fish lie!"

"Is that a moose?"

Usually I'd just smile. I didn't want to burst anyone's happiness balloon with the less glamorous details of the job. Hosing the boat down every evening. Staying up until the wee hours to tie half a dozen flies because that's the only fly that's working and if you don't tie 'em yourself, you're probably out of luck. Getting up early every morning to make a thermos of coffee for a mid-morning break. Always watching someone else fish, and seldom getting to fish yourself. Making a wage that, at its best, hovers in the lower ranks of middle management at your average Fortune 5000 corporation.

And floating the same two or three damn stretches of river day in, day out, for six months. To the point where you don't just know every rock in the river, but you know every rock and tree and bush and blade of grass on either bank. Have names for each of the river otters and beavers and deer and coyote that frequent each stretch. Can calculate exactly how long it will take to float from point A to point B, taking into account the variables of number of fish caught, wind speed, and likeliness of having to stop the boat to untangle my sports' leaders. Finding ways to make each day interesting to me—so I could make it fun and interesting for my sports—was the greatest challenge as the season wore on. One year, it was finding ways to plant a half-eaten—and slowly rotting—bagel in the cooler of fellow guides. The most inventive stowaway solution found the bagel secreted away in a Budweiser can that had been cut open, emptied, and soldered back together before being placed in the unwitting guide's cooler. It made for an unpleasant surprise for his client, who was looking to celebrate a brown trout he'd landed on a streamer. But as the guide explained the prank, the client was soon laughing too.

What makes a great day of guiding? And conversely, what makes a terrible day on the water? It's not the weather, or if the fish are biting, or if a certain bug is hatching, or how many people are on the water, or if you come upon a bull elk squared off with a mountain lion. It's about the client . . . or more precisely, it's about how clearly the client can express what they want to take away from the day, assuming their expectations are in the realm of reason. (An example of a less than reasonable desire: "I want to catch lots of big fish on small dry flies." My response: "Me too. But it's probably not going to happen.") Some clients want to catch lots of fish. It's all about numbers; more than a few have carried a clicker on board to tabulate their conquests, more interested in making sure they register their catch than marveling at its brilliant coloration. (No surprise there, the Blue being known for its vast numbers of trout.) For some guests, it's about quality, not quantity. They'd pass up twenty fish on a nymph rig to have a few good shots at one trophy fish on a dry fly—preferably a small one, though a large fly would do too. Still others delight in a nice boat ride and a chance to learn a bit about the natural history of the Blue and its surrounding environs. Occasionally, it's just an excuse to pound beers (though per state law, clients must provide their own alcohol, and that requires some planning around Belgian Flats if you like anything but Keystone Light).

If I can figure out what a client wants, nine times out of ten I can give them a good day. And that's what feels good to me. Sometimes it takes some drawing out to determine what my sports are after. Over time, I've become pretty good at doing so:

ME: How's your cast?

CLIENT: Pretty good.

TRANSLATION: Can cast the leader and maybe a dozen feet of line, with three or four false casts. Better keep things simple.

ME: Do you fish with guides much?

CLIENT: No. I don't really need a guide, just access to a boat as mine is back in _____ [state here].

TRANSLATION: Really needs lots of help if he hopes to catch any fish.

me: What brings you to fish the Blue?

CLIENT: I've always heard good things about it, and wanted to see it for myself.

TRANSLATION: Has an open mind and is ready for anything the day presents.

What does the ideal client look like? A teenager, old enough to have good hand-eye coordination, but young enough not to have started rejecting authority. Or pretty much any woman who's genuinely interested in giving fly fishing a try. Both parties come into the boat without lots of preconceptions (or ingrained bad habits) and take instruction well. When you see things suddenly click for them, it's like catching your first trout all over again. The wonder is back.

The monster client has lost any sense of wonder. Or proportion, for that matter. It's the guy—and it's almost always a guy—who, before you've even launched the boat, has rattled off a few of the bucket list destinations he's fished. He may drop a few names—infamous guides, writers, or other luminaries that he's fished with. If there's another angler with him, he will repeat any guidance I offer to make it his, or, more commonly, contradict anything that I say. (I especially pity his poor accomplice, as he must suffer the monster's blowhard company beyond our time on the water.) If there are fish rising at twenty feet and fifty feet from the boat, he'll choose the farther fish to highlight his casting skill . . . even though that means putting all the closer fish down. (When you point this out, he'll inform you that the closer fish were all "dinks," and he was going for the "hawg.") There's no question that the monster knows how to fish; his loops are tight, he mends with precision, and seldom misses a hook set. But there's a lingering sense that he relies on guides so much, he's forgotten how to think for himself. Without a guide, he'd likely be helpless.

The monster's worst features emerge when it comes time to chronicle his catch. Photographic evidence is necessary for every fish, from multiple angles, with the "grip and grin" front and center—even if that means ignoring Trout Unlimited's (and every other fish conservation group's) pleas to "Keep 'Em Wet." If I mention how holding a trout out of the water for a minute to get a picture is like holding a human's head under the water for a minute—not to mention the impact of human hands on the fish's skin—he'll sulk for a while and perhaps allow the next few fish to be released from the net without a photo shoot. But by the third fish, he's back to insisting on getting his shots . . . and implying that my tip for the day could be adversely affected if I say otherwise. I could care less about his crappy tip. But I don't come out on the water to have confrontations and can see the discomfort the conflict over the monster's snapshot mania is causing his hapless accomplice. So I back off . . . hating myself for my timidity.

Spend a day or two in the boat with the know-it-all monster client, and you might second-guess that decision to ditch your desk jockey job for the colorful world of guiding.

CHAPTER FIVE

Oligarchs and Trust Fund Punks

WHEN I RETURNED TO THE TABLE, JD WAS WORKING ON A SEC-ond plate of biscuits. I imagine they were an offering from Rita to assuage his earlier outburst.

"So, Cody," he said as I prepared to tuck into the cooling remains of my scrambled eggs. "We were talking about the future. Your future." He paused, then added, "Beyond the next month."

"I have to admit that I'm not the biggest planner," I offered. "But it sounds like you have some ideas. Which of course, I'd love to hear."

"I'm glad that you remain open-minded, Cody. That shows that there's still hope of avoiding the future I described before you adjourned for the shitter." At his mention of the future, I thought of Dickens's *A Christmas Carol* and pictured JD in the guise of the Ghost of Christmas Future, a tattered Simms rain jacket, and a Winston rod replacing the Dickensian ghost's cloak and scythe, respectively.

"As you might imagine, I've made a number of friends in the fly-fishing world over the years," JD said. "Sometimes they come to me when they're in need of counsel, or seeking key personnel to help them realize their dreams. Some of these friends, it's worth noting, are seated in chairs of considerable reach and power. Technology moguls, captains of legacy industries. Financiers.

Trust fund punks. Oligarchs in the developing world. Benevolent dictators. Sometimes I wonder why they'd put so much trust in a little old fishing guide from Belgian Flats."

I didn't believe that for a second. Then an inspiration struck me. "JD, I have a strong feeling there's going to be a nice BWO hatch soon. Why don't we take this conversation out to the river? I'll row."

If my temerity surprised him, JD didn't let it show. He tucked a twenty under his plate and started toward the door, calling out to no one in particular, "Let's go rip some lips."

CHAPTER SIX

Prissy Brits

THE FEW GUIDES MALINGERING AROUND THE PUT-IN ON SEC-tion One looked surprised as I dropped my boat in and JD vaulted into the front. Joe Lampres lost the grip on the forty-ouncer that helped him greet each day, the glass shattering in a circle.

"Make sure you clear that up, Jojo," JD called as I pushed us off. "I find any glass in my tires, I'm gonna cut your ass with it." Joe hustled toward the dumpster to find some cardboard to help sweep up the remnants of his Old Gold, though his hustle was more a crab crawl, as he had bad hips; I'd heard he'd broken them both in the rodeo, though it could've been a car crash or a degenerative disorder.

We hadn't floated more than fifty yards before I saw a few heads poking up through a foam line that paralleled the left bank. My instincts about a Blue Winged Olive hatch had been correct, and I dropped anchor. I didn't have to point the fish out to JD. He peeled a few loops of line off the reel, dumped it in the river on the right side, let the current straighten it out, and dropped his fly, a little Sparkle Dun by the looks of it, five feet above the nearest fish with an effortless water load cast. A head rose up to meet the fly and with the slightest grunt, JD lifted. He quickly played the fish in, a modest rainbow, and popped the hook out with his own version of the Ketchum Release tool, which resembled a dental instrument.

"Let me pluck off one or two more and then you can have at it," he said, delicately dropping his fly above the next fish in the foam. Soon another grunt and lift. This was a better fish, a brown I'd guess, as it bulldogged toward the bottom. JD was nonchalant, holding his rod above his head as line slowly click-clicked off his reel, a vintage Hardy. In his huge hands the rod seemed tiny, like some sort of 1-weight novelty outfit you'd find in the back of a fly-fishing catalog. JD bided his time and the fish came in. This one he netted before popping out the hook. I noticed that his lips were moving as he looked down at the fish, though no words were audible. Perhaps he was giving a blessing . . . or a curse.

"Make a few casts, Cody, and I'll paint a small picture of the future that might await you." I rigged up one of the client 5-weights I left in the boat, a fast-action cheapo that was easy for newbies to work with. JD fished a can of Sierra Nevada from somewhere in his coat and popped the top, sending a spray of pale ale into the late morning air. "It's happy hour somewhere," he said. The fish to the left had gone down after the brown came to hand, but there were more snouts downstream. I pulled in the anchor so we could float into them.

A few downstream drifts brought two nice rainbows to hand. "Let me see that," JD said, gesturing at my fly. I dangled it in front of him and he snipped off my little Baetis and tied on one of his beloved purple Chubby Chernobyls. "If you wanna catch big fish, you gotta use a big bait," he said. "Now let that thing swing into the fish. No mending." The fly gurgled and dragged and whipped through the patch of water where the trout had been blurping. It was hard to believe that they hadn't seen it; such an aberration should have sent them tearing toward the bottom. "Again," JD snapped. "Mend it downstream so that mother really rips through there." The Chubby whipped along, resembling nothing in the trout's day-to-day diet. As I prepared to flip the fly into the boat to change it up, a wake appeared behind the Chubby and the fish sucked it under with a sound like the flushing of an old-school toilet. I set the hook and my rod bent double. Those of us who fish the Blue regularly get to know where the big trout lie; in fifteen years, I'd never encountered a rainbow like this here. My reel was screaming, and the fish leaped clear of the water fifty yards downstream. And then it was gone.

"Gotta bow the rod to those big guys. Like tarpon," JD said.

"Huh?"

"Bow the rod. Tip it to the water. Gives 'em a little slack so it's harder to throw the hook. Haven't you ever fished for tarpon? Did you break him off?" The bug was still attached, skipping along the surface as I reeled in. "Nope," I replied.

"Perhaps we should float a bit so I can enlighten you about my proposition, undisturbed?" I brought the anchor in and we floated. There were few boats around, and no "bankies"—wading anglers who hiked up and down Section One to find feeding fish, and who seemed to delight in provoking guides and sports in driftboats. JD produced two more Sierras from inside his jacket and I accepted one.

"It's a fine morning beer," he said to no one in particular. "So Cody—have you ever been to the Federated States of Russia? The former Soviet Union?"

"I have not," I replied, "though I've heard a little bit about the fishing."

"There are a wonder of angling opportunities behind the so-called Red Curtain," JD said, spinning his seat around so he was facing me, with his Topsiders—the only shoes I ever saw him wear—just to the left of my rowing seat. Given his tone and the position of relative comfort he'd assumed, I imagined this would be a longer soliloquy. "In a country some six thousand miles in length—encompassing eleven time zones—you can imagine that there are a number of fisheries that have not garnered the attention of the outside world, perhaps not even the curiosity of the oligarch class centered around greater Moscow. For now, the eyes of the angling world have settled on the two farthest reaches of the republic: the Kola Peninsula in the northwest, and the Kamchatka Peninsula in the Far East." After a few prodigious slurps, he continued.

"The possibilities of the Kola Peninsula were first explored by anglers in the late 1980s, just as the forces of Soviet-style communism were shuddering in their death throes. Rivers near Murmansk—home of Russia's Northern Fleet, if you're not a student of the great European Conflict—were found to have prolific runs of Atlantic salmon. Some rivers held fish that might eclipse forty pounds. Exploration to the southern extremes of the peninsula, led in part by the graphite rod pioneer Gerald Lordes, revealed what is now considered to be the world's most fecund Atlantic salmon river, the Pototanga. Since that time, camps of varying quality have been constructed, torn down and reconstructed on the Pototanga, which caters largely to British anglers of a certain age who have very few salmon of their own left in Great Britain."

A hundred yards or so downstream, an adolescent bull moose that the guide corps had collectively named Bullwinkle waded uneasily into the river. Whether it was seeking a snack of aquatic vegetation or a cool drink was hard to discern. I found myself wondering if young moose were ever exposed to grandiloquent, mildly pedantic older moose, and if so, how they escaped them without bruising any feelings.

"Kamchatka came on the adventure angling map around the same time," JD continued, as Bullwinkle, finally noticing our presence, ambled slowly back into the willows. "First it was steelhead, a fishing program pioneered by conservation organizations such as The Wild Salmon Center, who figured out a clever weasel that would allow visiting anglers to write off a good portion of their exorbitant trip expense. Later came the discovery of amazing trout streams, filled with rainbows that could easily be mistaken for steelhead, save for their vivid coloration. Some said it was like Alaska fifty years ago. Though fifty years ago, many of Alaska's most storied rainbow streams had not even been discovered. So I think those comparing Kamchatka to Alaska have not properly considered what they are saying.

"Of course, the Russian fisheries have faced some unique challenges. The vagaries of political fortune, for starters. And the inclination of Russian outfitters—particularly those in the eastern reaches of the vast nation—to see hard-won and, it should be mentioned, *pre-paid* contracts—as fungible, evolving documents. And the tendency of commercial airlines to initiate service to Murmansk and Petropavlovsk, respectively, and cancel said service on a whim. But if the stars align, regimes maintain power, and the dollar and pound retain their relative strength vis-à-vis the Russian ruble, some fine fishing can be had." Downstream, a new pod of working fish appeared on river right, and I prepared to drop anchor so, if nothing else, I could consider what JD had shared thus far.

"You wanna throw the Chubby?" I said, reaching for my rod so I could hand it off.

"*El Chubblito* would likely work," JD said, picking up his own rod. "But I like to save that for special occasions. For the bigger fish that might not respond to more modest proposals. The sparkle thingy I have will be enough." Without even looking at the rise forms, he flung a cast over his shoulder, landing the fly three feet above the nearest riser. He turned in time to set the hook when the fish came up.

"Hmm!"

The fish, like so many on the Blue, seemed to understand that the torture we were inflicting upon him would be greatly lessened if he simply lay on his side and let himself be ratcheted in. Reaching the boat, he even seemed to turn on his back to present the fly more directly, thus facilitating his release.

"I believe it is the Kola Peninsula that is calling you now, young Cody, a clarion call that you'd be well-advised to consider very carefully," he said, somehow producing two more Sierra cans from his jacket—was there a miniature cooler built into its pockets? Two more "whooshes" and I was soon on my way to a good noontime buzz. JD held his can to his ear. "What's that? Yes, he's here." He put his hand over the can and whispered, "It's Russia." Tilting the can toward his mouth, he said, "Yes, he's amenable to the notion. Yes, I'll get back to you. *Dasvidaniya*."

JD turned to me without missing a beat. "The proposal is a good one, in my estimation. It will be a not inconsiderable reach for you in terms of your existing skill set, but one that I have little doubt you will rise to. And the new skills you gain will leave you eminently prepared for an elevated future in the sporting profession. And perhaps other areas of endeavor. What do you say?"

"I was hoping for a little more detail before I commit."

"That does not seem an unreasonable request." JD cast his little BWO straight downstream, not bothering to mend or otherwise attempt to give the fly a natural appearance. It bounced in the current as he cleared his throat and continued.

"There is an esteemed Atlantic salmon lodge on the Kola Peninsula, Cody, on the aforementioned Pototanga, that has recently lost its camp host. My understanding is that he was a bright young man and a fine angler from the United Kingdom, but showed a bit too much enthusiasm for vodka. And for the younger—and presumably bored—wives of the older anglers that the lodge tends to cater to. He was asked to leave at the end of the fall season. The gentleman that owns the lodge—a well-heeled oligarch, not unlike those I may have mentioned earlier—has reached out to me as someone whom he considers a well-informed member of the fly-fishing community or brotherhood, to suggest potential replacements. Perhaps it was his subtle way of asking if *I'd* be willing to consider the post myself. A man such as he doesn't get to such a status in life without playing the angles." There was a loud splash and JD pivoted downstream. His rod was pulsing, and the ancient Hardy roared as if it might take flight any second.

"Sometimes I wish these Blue River fish would show at least a modicum of discretion," he muttered. "Cody, would you untether us so I can recover my fly?" One of the rumors that circulated about JD was that he hated to part with flies, even though he was sent cartons of them by commercial tiers hoping he'd give them a plug. Perhaps it was true. The fish put on a good game for a while, pulling downstream toward a bouldery patch where a sharp rock could pop the tippet. But as we floated down on her and JD gained back line, she began to dog down and give up the ghost. I dropped anchor and brought out the net. It was a brown, an immense hen. Though I didn't put the tape to her, I guessed she'd measure out at twenty-six or twenty-eight inches, a real trophy anywhere, especially on the Blue. JD was nonplussed. "Be careful with the net, Cody," he said, an unfamiliar hint of anxiety in his voice. "I don't want to part with that bug." For a moment I considered letting the net slide out of my hands, which would likely tangle the tippet in the webbing, thus parting ways between the fly in the brown's jaw and JD. But not wanting to cancel my trip to Russia before it had begun, I swung the net to JD and he plucked the fly free with his little tool. "Back to daddy," he murmured, nipping the little Sparkle dun and popping it into his shirt pocket. Having his fly back seemed to bring JD a bit of calm, and he closed his eyes as I pulled up anchor.

"So the Russian lodge is looking for a manager, and you think I might make a good candidate?" I asked, trying to steer JD back from whatever reverie the recovery of his fly had inspired. "Why do you think I might be good match?"

He slowly batted his eyes in the manner of a waking lizard, and said, "Equanimity." He drifted away again. I was becoming slightly infuriated with what I saw as an inconsistent attention to my future. Spying an exposed rock downstream, I steered the boat in its direction. The concussion was enough to jar him back to the living, and he continued without missing a beat.

"I haven't been in your boat day-in/day-out, Cody. But I've noticed that on the water and off, you're rather unflappable. That is an important quality when overseeing a crew of forty or fifty deep in the taiga. Especially when they are catering to a prissy group of Brits. But I digress. Not only are you a calming presence, Cody, but you're young. Young enough to put your shoulder against the metaphoric wheel, as they say, and not be too much worse for the wear. But not so young as to be green behind the ears and make the sort of mistake that could earn you the disdain of your staff, like getting caught schtupping the barmaid from Murmansk in the supply closet. You're also educated. Cultivated. At least somewhat. In a pinch, you could discuss a Hemingway story. Or P. G. Wodehouse. And tell the difference between a pistachio and a Picasso. These people may be prissy, but they are urbane . . . or like to think themselves so. You can be at ease with them. But you can also manage the rabble, as it were. And the nuclear physicists reduced to guiding because the so-called communist government rewards physicists a stipend the equivalent of \$50/month, which they might earn in tips in one day on the river.

"In terms of compensation, you needn't worry. My Russian will expect you to work hard and run a tight ship, but is quite prepared to reward you handsomely for your efforts. You will earn enough between May and mid-October to live quite well the rest of the year—even more so as you'll have zero living expenses while ensconced at the lodge. You will be rubbing shoulders—figuratively, at least in most cases—with the sort of people who can afford a \$15,000/week fishing vacation without a thought. Should your future interests tend toward the world of high finance or industry, these men wield the sort of influence that could land you a plum position in the time it takes to punch a phone number. Or have their man punch a phone number, as they are not typically technically inclined. But they can chat about the pros and cons of the Hardy Marquis versus the Princess versus the Perfect versus the work of Stan Bogdan, and you can no doubt hold your own in that vein of conversation, and likewise in your consumption of gin and hearty red wines. Yes, vodka is the lingua franca of the land, but many Brits will bring their Boodles and Hendricks and want to share, quietly suggesting that vodka is fine for the Russians, but, well, a bit *coarse*, don't you think?

"Should this opportunity be of interest—and by the look on your face, young Cody, I would say that your curiosity is piqued—I will arrange a brief teleconference with the powers that be. That would include Dmitri, the aforementioned owner. And Mr. Quinones, an Ecuadorian national who, the best that I can tell, serves as Dmitri's man on the ground. This will be largely a formality. Providing that you smile, speak in the King's English, and refrain from any overt acts of sexual perversity, you will be granted the position on the weight of my recommendation alone."

We were nearing the last mile of the Section One float, and fish were rising on all sides of the boat. Blue Winged Olives, I supposed, though given JD's earlier catch, the fish might have been rising to cottonwood seeds. They really weren't very particular.

"Do you want to make a few more casts, JD?"

"My appetite is sated, Cody," he replied, producing another two cans of pale ale from inside his jacket. "With fish, anyway."

Chapter Seven

A Psychic Break

When I dropped JD back at Rita's, we agreed that I would get back to him the day after Thanksgiving about whether I wished to pursue the lodge management position in Russia. "Don't give this number to anyone else, Cody," he said, pressing a crumpled piece of paper into my palm. "It's my private line." I imagined a red phone in the shape of a trout, hidden behind the fake wood panels of some single-wide. Or maybe built into the dash of the F-350.

I had an afternoon to think about the season that had passed before my last client of the season arrived. Some of my long-time clients, I must admit, had me stocking up on Tums, ibuprofen, and infinite dry bags of patience. Had it been practical, I might have printed the Serenity Prayer on the bottom of the visor of my go-to ball cap (which bears the logo of the floatant brand Fly Agra). Yet the multiday trips they booked made up the core of my business, as much as one could call it such. They could alternatingly be arrogant, ignorant, incompetent, avaricious, infantile, and, if copious amounts of alcohol were introduced, downright repugnant. But their checks didn't bounce. Thanks in part to their patronage, the tiny shingle I'd hung on the Blue, "Fishing with Cody," floated on.

Kennon Bliss was different. For starters, he knew how to fish. He could roll cast, steeple cast, cast off his left shoulder or his right, and single-hand spey cast if necessary. He could tie on his own flies, and *tie* his own flies . . . and knew what he needed to tie for his visits without texting me a dozen times beforehand. He could row a boat through Class III rapids and hold it in a slick without disturbing feeding fish, and didn't mind doing so to provide me with a few casting opportunities, even though he was footing the bill.

Bliss was also an educated man, with an inquiring mind, curious about many topics—politics, literature (high and low), music (old and new), business trends. But he didn't feel the need to bludgeon you with his knowledge. Instead, he would slide his observations in delicately after another opinion—most likely less eloquent and more shoddily reasoned—had been offered. He seemed to understand that a good day on the water did not directly correlate to the number of fish, the presence of big fish, an encounter with a curious bear or moose, or the brilliance of a sunrise or sunset—but some intangible combination of all of these factors and more.

Yes, he was a valued client. But he was also a friend.

I'd been lucky to have booked Kennon Bliss as my last client of the year for the past three seasons. A few days in the boat with him could rectify the psychic pain inflicted by some of my lesser clients, and steel me to forge ahead into the following year. The first day we floated Section One. Just like the day before, Blue Winged Olives were out, sailing along like tiny little schooners, only to be engulfed by the mouths of hungry trout—little Moby-Dicks sinking their *Pequod*s, as it were. I pulled the boat opposite pods of feeding fish and anchored up; Kennon would pick off the fish one by one, working from the outside in. Before lunch, he'd landed at least twenty, an even mix of browns and rainbows. After pulling over opposite a pool that hadn't turned on yet (but I was confident would with a bump in the air temp), I set out the sandwiches that Rita had prepared; she was the main purveyor of lunches for the Belgian Flats guide corps.

"What do we have today?" Kennon asked.

"Ham and cheese." I could say this with confidence without unfolding the kraft paper they came wrapped in, as ham and cheese was the only sandwich that Rita offered. If you happened to abstain from pork, you got cheese. If you were vegan, you got bread, tomato, sweet pickles and lettuce. If you were gluten-free, you were out of luck.

"Has Rita received her first Michelin Star?" Kennon asked, while smearing one of the gourmet mustards I carried in the boat to liven up our entrees on his bread. After a bite he asked, "Been listening to any new music?"

"Not really."

"I've been rediscovering Pavement."

Growing up in Baker, I had not been privy to cutting-edge music developments. We had one classic rock station, and its programming director studiously avoided anything the least bit edgy or imaginative. It also seemed that most of the material in their rotation came from second-tier bands from the '70s and '80s. In a given hour, you could always count on a few hits from Styx, Kansas, Boston, and REO Speedwagon. Beatles and Stones songs were few and far between; forget about the Clash or Jefferson Airplane. A friend from Missoula had a theory about this: He reasoned that record companies cut stations in smaller, remote media markets a special royalty deal on the second-rate material. This damned their listeners to an eternal cycle of lower musical mediocrity. My musical education had a lot of catching up to do by the time I arrived at college. And though there was certainly some good new music coming out in the early '90s, I was still cycling through Dylan's *Blonde on Blonde* and the Velvet Underground.

"I remember more about the people who fancied themselves Pavement fans than the band itself," I finally said. "They were the guys who looked down on almost everything. Except the Beach Boys album *Pet Sounds*." I imagine that most of them aspired to be music critics at alternative weeklies in Boulder or Berkeley, and were now blogging in their underwear from their mothers' basements.

"I can see that. They are a little precious. But I like their grooves. And the guitar player is pretty good."

"I enjoy the hair-cutting song."

"That's a good one," Kennon said, flicking a crust into the river. It floated two yards before being scarfed my a largish rainbow. "I find that I'll be enjoying a song, and then some guy starts screaming like an idiot. And I have to turn it off. There are enough screaming idiots in the world. I don't need another one on my stereo."

I couldn't argue with that logic.

CHAPTER EIGHT

Carpe Diem

When I picked up Kennon at the Belgian Quarters—the burg's one motel, and default residence of most angling visitors—he had a funny smirk on his face. "I have something a little different in mind today," he said, dropping a quiver of rods in the back of my truck. "Do you mind if I drive?" I did not, and we swapped places.

Instead of turning left at the bridge that spanned the retaining wall of the reservoir that made the Blue possible, Kennon turned right. Soon we were cruising along Blue Lake. Most visitors to the Blue didn't realize that without the dam, there would be no blue-ribbon trout fishery. And very few if any trout. Before the dam, the Blue ran warm and muddy in the summer, far too warm to sustain cold-water species like trout. It was the domain of catfish and carp. The dam no doubt interfered with the natural flow of the Blue, no longer permitting rocks and silt to move downstream during spring runoff and interfering with the historic movements of its native fishes. Though the long-term environmental consequences of the dam on the Blue are still to be seen, the short-term results have been positive for those who favor the long rod. The cold water that it stores at the bottom of Blue Lake and releases gradually throughout the year is the *only* reason a trout fishery exists here. Anyone who rails indiscriminately against dams might want to first check and see if their favorite stream flows out from under one; chances are good that it does.

As we drove farther and farther from the Blue's celebrated trout waters, Kennon painted a picture of the day he'd planned. "Everyone understands the appeal of trout," he began. "They take little flies on the surface. They are beautiful to behold with their dots and splashes of color. And some of them even jump. But we are reaching a time where the waters that can support trout are fewer and farther between. For most Americans, trout streams are not a leisurely hour or two drive away but demand an all-night road trip or air travel. So—do most of us hang up our fly rods save for the three long weekends a year when we can find the time or money to get away? Or do we begin to look elsewhere for our fun?" He slowed my rig and pulled left into a picnic area that included a small boat launch. "Today, Cody," he continued, "we are fishing for carp!"

This was not the first I'd heard of the fly-fishing-for-carp phenomenon. A few of the younger Blue River guides were crazy for it, heading up to the lake at every opportunity:

"You see them coming from fifty yards away, it's such a rush!"

"They're picky as hell. One muffed cast and they're out of there. Pickier than permit!"

"They're huge! And they pull like a salmon!"

And so on. Still, I had trouble getting past my initial impression of carp fishing, from a boyhood trip with my family to the Brownlee Reservoir on the Snake River where it separates Oregon from Idaho. There, I watched a group of bedraggled men who might have once been called hobos baiting treble hooks with a stinky blend of jello mix and canned cat food, and flinging their heavily weighted baits into the murky flows beyond the spillway. They'd then set the rods into a forked stick and wait, as they made their way through an immense assemblage of Busch Light cans. Not a terribly engaging way to fish, at least to my tastes.

And there was also the question of the carp's appearance. Their heavy body, oversized scales, little mouth, and drab color- ation—particularly the pale, sickly white of their bellies—were a stark contrast to the sleekly proportioned, brightly hued rainbow trout that consumed most of my fishing reveries. Beauty is, of course, a social construct, and rests in the eyes of the beholder; but my constructs would have to be seriously revised to see beauty in the carp. I really didn't even want to touch them.

But touch them I would.

Using Google Earth, Kennon had identified some shallows a short row from the put-in. Though the lake could be slightly murky with algae at the height of summer, it was clear now with the brisk fall weather. The morning was cool but calm, and Kennon anchored the boat so the sun was behind us, optimizing our ability to spot our prey cruising for breakfast. He put me in the front of the boat and handed me an 8-weight rigged with a crayfish pattern. I'd heard that carp were Catholic eaters, feeding on insects, minnows, crustaceans, and even certain berries. "This is no country for 5-weights," he said with mock solemnity. Had we been in the Caribbean, Kennon would have propelled us along with a long graphite pole from a tall platform above our skiff's outboard engine. Since we lacked a skiff, an outboard engine and a push pole, he climbed onto the rower's seat to better scan the flats before us. For anyone driving by who knew anything about fly fishing, we must have seemed like Bahamian bonefishermen who'd badly lost their way. "We'll use the clock system," he continued.

"Twelve is front, three to your right, et cetera, et cetera," I replied.

"You're a quick study."

I stripped out some fly line and dropped it across the prow of my boat, hoping it wouldn't tangle around the leg braces. I had ten feet of fly line outside of the rod tip along with the leader and the fly between my thumb and index finger, so I could start a cast quickly. We didn't have to wait very long.

"I've got a fish at ten o'clock, moving to the right, about fifty feet," Kennon whispered. "I'd drop the fly at noon, now." My heart was pumping more than I would've imagined. It took me an extra back cast to get the proper amount of line out—I was rusty with the 8-weight—and instead of landing in front of the fish, the crawfish dropped above the carp's head. The fish bolted for deeper water, leaving a cloud of sand in its wake.

"Maybe you should try to get it a little closer," Kennon said dryly. "Normally you'd be done. But as it's your first time, I'll give you another crack." A cloud that resembled a zebra passed over the low-hanging sun and our visibility went to hell. My fingers started to get cold, and I was beginning to think that I'd blown my one shot for the day. But as the sun returned, Kennon giggled.

"We have a veritable armada of fish coming from the right. You can't miss. They're at two o'clock now, about forty feet. There are six, eight of them. Do you have them?" I nodded; it would be hard not to see eighty-odd pounds of carp swimming along, their silverish backs standing out against the white sand.

"Give me forty feet at 12:30." With one backcast I dropped the fly in the general region of 12:30.

"Am I a little long?"

"That's okay. Give it a bump. They'll see it." I gave the fly a little strip. The lead fish swerved in the fly's direction, then turned away.

"Another pop," Kennon whispered. When the fly moved this time, a fish toward the back of the string moved in its direction and sucked the crayfish pattern in.

"Strip set! Don't lift!"

Somehow I remembered not to do the "trout set"—lifting the rod tip up and effectively pulling the fly away from the fish—and instead pulled back on the line with my left hand. I was tight to my first carp.

"Damn!" I cried as the reel handle spun against my knuckles. "They do pull hard." I tightened down the drag on Kennon's reel as the fish tore toward the deeper water, then cut back across the shallows. The fish wasn't *quite* as fast as a steelhead nor quite as *strong* as a big Louisiana bull redfish, but I was impressed. After five minutes, I had it to the boat, resting in the oversized net that Kennon had brought along.

"Time for a picture," he said, beaming.

"Do I have to?"

"Evidence for posterity."

I leaned over and placed my hands beneath the fish's belly. As I lifted, I held my breath, as I was convinced the fish would stink. The photo Kennon took and later mailed along, blown up and framed, shows me scowling more than smiling, as if I were holding someone's used colostomy bag. The legend he'd added in an elegant calligraphy on the border below the photo: "A Boy's First Carp."

CHAPTER NINE

Something's Brewing in Baker

THE DAY AFTER KENNON DEPARTED, I GATHERED UP MY BELONG-ings—not a strenuous task, given my nomadic lifestyle at the time—stashed my boat behind a friend's double-wide, and headed west. I'd be driving right past some of America's greatest trout streams as I made my way to Baker, and not all of them were closed for the season. But I'd had my fill of trout and then some. I wanted a crack at some ocean-going fish—steelhead, to be precise. But I needed to visit my parents first, at least for a few days. So I rose early, barreled across Utah and Idaho, only stopping for gas and coffee, and rolled into Baker just after dinner time. The dinner table was set, and my mom was at the front door as I approached. "We weren't very hungry," she assured me, though I knew that was a bald lie; even in retirement, dinner was on the table every night at six o'clock, and done by 6:15. I was their only child, and the apple—albeit one permeated with worms—of their collective eye. The prodigal son had returned, and the fatted calf (or in this case, a lasagna, my favorite meal) had been prepared.

As we made our way through small talk (How was the drive? Was the last month busy? Did you pack some dollars away?), I could feel the "what the heck are you doing with your life" hammer beginning to drop. But it was a velvet hammer at worst. My dad had worked as a CPA with the same local firm all of his adult life, and still helped friends and neighbors with their taxes in his retirement. He thrived on routine and certainty, everything in its proper time and place. I don't think he hated the idea of me working as fishing guide so much as it was utter anathema, something he couldn't begin to understand. People pay enough to go fishing for you to make a living? You don't know from week to week whether you'll have a day of work or not? Being outside of his realm of his experience or imagination, it scared him. And he couldn't quite comprehend that it didn't scare me.

"Another season, done eh?" he asked, daintily sopping up some tomato sauce that remained on his plate with a slice of the premade garlic bread that Mom always kept in the freezer just in case. "Still enjoying it?"

I weighed my response carefully. If I said it was going well, he might take my response as a rejection of all he stood for. If I said it was getting a little old, that might give him an in to pitch his old firm's management training program, as he still had contacts there and I could fish every weekend if I wanted to. I opted for a middle path. "It's alright," I said, noticing that mom was perched on the edge of her chair, as if awaiting her verdict on a Class A felony. "There are good days and bad days, like any other job, I guess."

"Though you haven't really had any other jobs," Dad murmured, almost to his napkin.

"Bill," Mom said sternly. I heard the muffled thud of her clog hitting Dad's shin.

"It really depends on who I have in the boat on a given day," I continued, skipping over Dad's dig and scooping a third slice of lasagna onto my plate. (There had been a lot of ramen the last few days in Belgian Flats.) "Even if the fishing's not great, good clients can make it a fun day."

"Did you make any new friends this summer?" Mom ventured, "friends" meaning lady friends. A career (and much loved) first grade teacher, she'd been ready for grandchildren since I finished college. I didn't think that my Halloween acquaintance was exactly what she had in mind . . . nor the one evening spent with a guide friend's sister as she passed through town toward a summer gig working on a dude ranch near Jackson.

"Mom, you've been to Belgian Flats. There aren't too many eligible young women in town. And not too many younger female anglers visiting either." Mom released a long sigh, dreams of trips to the mall with little Sierra or Sebastian floating away with her exhalation.

"You know best," she said, adding in a whisper, "I suppose."

"Are you booking clients for next season?" Dad ventured, exploring a different angle.

"Not yet." Though it was premature, I decided to float JD's Russian proposition, as it might brighten their spirits, seeing that it pointed to a small elevation in my employment status. "You see, I've been asked to consider a position managing a well-known lodge in Russia. On the Kola Peninsula, near Finland. They have a very well-heeled clientele, apparently. One of my fellow guides at Belgian Flats is well-connected in the fishing world, and he recommended me to the owner, a wealthy Russian. I'll have to do an interview, but I've been led to believe that it's a formality, and the job is mine if I want it." I thought the announcement of my leap into the management ranks would bring my folks some level of comfort, yet it seemed to have the opposite effect.

"Will you be paid in rubles?" Dad asked.

"What if they take your passport?" Mom added.

"What if diplomatic relations break down?" Dad returned.

"Will you meet Putin?" Mom volleyed back.

Finally, I held my arms up. "Nothing's finalized. I have to think about it. And I'll have a call sometime after Thanksgiving with the owner. Can I clear the dishes?"

I stayed in Baker a few more days, helping my folks with chores during the day and catching up with a few high school buddies at night. It wasn't hard to find them, as not many had left town. With the advent of high-speed internet, more and more city folks had relocated to Baker seeking, I suppose, a slice of the country life. A new brewpub had opened, a sign of the slowly changing times, though Baker was in no danger of becoming the next Sun Valley or Bend. Nonetheless, the pub brewed an exceptional IPA. The topic of Russia didn't come up again at home, and on day three I loaded the car again to go fishing.

CHAPTER TEN

Bondo on the Rondo

ONE GOOD THING ABOUT BEING A FISHING GUIDE IS THAT YOU get to know lots of other fishing guides in different places. They come and fish your river when their season isn't happening, and you take care of them—a sofa to crash on, a quick float when your guide day is done, the borrow of a rod or even a boat. They'll reciprocate when you show up on their river. Having grown up in Oregon, I knew a little bit about the Columbia Basin's steelhead rivers—when to fish them, and where. But as any angler will tell you, there's nothing like up-to-the-minute local intel. I'd made a few calls, and the inside line pointed to the Grande Ronde as the Pacific Northwest's best steelhead bet. That's where I headed.

The Grande Ronde has many commendable qualities—the beauty of its steep canyons, a blend of basalt faces and pine forests dotted with larch and aspens; its many well-defined runs, ideal for spey casters eager to swing flies; and the easy accessibility of most of those runs by the road that adjoins the river from above Troy on the Oregon side to Boggan's Oasis in Washington—settlements not unlike Belgian Flats, but even smaller. The steelhead may not be as chrome bright as the fish you might encounter further down the Columbia, as they've traveled some four hundred miles from the salt, gaining several thousand feet of elevation along the way. But they still account for themselves well, especially the natives that arrive in October. Some people fish the later hatchery arrivals into the dead of winter. If you enjoy frozen fingers and playing old boots on your 7- or 8-weight, have at it. Not something of interest to me.

I knew a few guides that periodically worked the Ronde, but my favorite was Bondo. Bondo claimed to have been a roadie for the Grateful Dead back in the day, though when I did the math, it didn't quite seem to add up . . . unless he was with the band as a toddler. "I was Bobby's guitar tech for a while, man," he'd shared the first time we fished together, referencing Bob Weir, the band's rhythm guitarist, who was always second fiddle to Jerry Garcia (at least in terms of guitarists). Bondo explained that his current name evolved from John Doe, which the other roadies called him when he joined his first tour as they could never recall his given name. John Doe became Bondo when he was farmed out to take care of Bob's guitar. True or not, it was a nice story, and apportioned well with his future part-time vocation as a steelhead guide.

"I'm Bondo on the Rondo. Get it?"

I got it.

Bondo was six feet tall and couldn't have topped 125 pounds soaking wet. He seemed to subsist on a diet of coffee, Mountain Dew, and cigarettes. When he was wading the river during bigger flows, I was afraid he'd be swept away. But he was wiry, and his tiny frame didn't provide much resistance to the water, which may have compensated for his lack of mass. When I'd offer him a can of beer or a puff on a joint (a vice I reserve for steelhead fishing), he'd always politely decline. His diet suggested the regimen of a reformed addict of one kind or another, but I didn't pry. One addiction replaces another for some personalities, and steelhead angling certainly qualifies as an addiction.

Sometimes the topic of steelhead fishing came up with clients on the Blue. Driving back and forth across the West and north into British Columbia—and stepping and casting countless hours on the Ronde, the Deschutes, the John Day, the Klickitat, the North

Umpqua, the Nehalem, the Queets, the Morice, and the Bulkley—I've had lots of time think about it. In fact, one long summer night in Belgian Flats, sick of tying flies and bored by whatever I was reading, I decided to try my hand at some automatic writing on the subject of steelhead. It might have worked better had I access to bourbon or peyote to fuel my stream-of-consciousness scrivening. As things were, my writing session was accompanied by several lukewarm mugs of chamomile tea:

The tug. Many hours of casting. Carry a loop. Don't carry a loop. Straight out. 45 degrees. 30 degrees. The drug. Same speed as a walking pace. Do nothing. Don't set. Don't do anything. Dark sky, light fly. Light sky, dark fly. Dark sky, dark fly? Mend once. Mend, mend. Don't mend. Any fly as long as it's a _____ (your fly here). Two flies—confidence and doesn't matter. Skaters work. Skaters don't work. Skaters work sometimes. Fish the tailouts. Fish the nervous water. Fish the riffles. Fish the runs. Fish the heads. Skip the heads. Fish a loop knot. Never fish a loop knot. Nymphing's not steelhead fishing. Nymphers suck. Nymphing works. The tug is the drug. Fish of a thousand casts. Fish of a million casts. No damn fish here. It was hot yesterday. It was hot last week. Check your gages. Never fish behind someone. Fish behind them if you cast better. I always catch fish behind people. Water needs to be clear. 3 foot of viz is fine. Foot of viz is enough. You won't catch any fish on your couch. They're chrome. They're unicorns. Oncorhynchus mykiss. They're mystical. They don't exist. Sea lice. Old boot. Greased lightning. Snakey. Kelt. Downstreamer. Set to shore. Do nothing. Let 'em turn the reel. Hit 'em. Felt the hook. Didn't prick him. 3 steps upstream. Smaller fly. Larger fly. Different fly. Same fly. Before a storm. After a storm. During a storm. More likely to get snakebit. More likely to get hit by lightning. You'll light 'em up. First light. Last light. Don't ignore mid-day. Let the water warm. Let it cool down. Let it dangle. Give it a pump. Be ready when you strip back. Spey rods are the way to go. Spey rods are for pussies who can't cast. Catch 'em any way you can.

The longest wait. The longest 3 seconds. Days and days of nothing. A test of patience. A test of endurance. The tug is the drug.

If clients pressed for my opinion on steelheading, I'd say it was a tough game, but a thrill if and when you hooked one.

Bondo lived in a canvass elk hunting tent in the little RV park that made up most of downtown Troy. The tent had seen better days. The roof was discolored in places, signs of numerous leaks, which explained its prevailing musty odor. You didn't need finely tuned hearing to detect the rustling of mice (and perhaps other vermin) in the shadows. But there was an aged cast iron stove to warm the tent through the cold autumn nights, one bare bulb to eat (and perhaps read) by, and simple bunks to house you and your sleeping bag. Given the shortcomings of Bondo's accommodations, and the limits of our conversational palate (the Grateful Dead and steelhead fishing), I tried to stay on the water as long as I could.

This wasn't hard. In early November, the fishing is sunup to sundown. The already long odds are stacked even further against you if the sun is on the water. Even on bright days, the sun's fall angle, combined with the Ronde's steep canyons, keep the light off the water on some runs if you look hard enough. And when the water is in the low 40s—as it often is in early November—the fish aren't moving much toward the surface anyway.

I liked fishing with Bondo. He didn't talk much, and had a great selection of Grateful Dead bootlegs, mostly on cassette tape. His silence and the Dead's often elliptical conflations combined with the Ronde's dramatic scenery helped induce a dreamy state as we drove up and down the river searching for unoccupied runs. This was ideal for steelhead fishing. (The occasional toke didn't hurt either.) You needed to pay *some* attention to cast and keep your footing on the slippery substrate. But *too* much attention, and you tense up. Too much tension and you're almost sure to jerk the rod if a fish ever shows up. I always admired Bondo's approach.

After casting and making one mend, he held his rod arm slackly at his side. It looked as though the rod might tumble out of his hand into the river it at any moment. "Monkey arms, Cody," he described it. "You don't see a monkey getting all stressed out." I *had* seen monkeys pretty stressed out on National Geographic programs, usually when leopards were around. And a zookeeper friend in Boston had shared how some monkeys would poop in their hand and throw it at attendants they didn't like.

Nonetheless, Bondo's technique was solid. When you've got monkey arms, it's pretty hard to do anything very quickly. Just what you want when a steelhead grabs a swung fly. *Do nothing.*

Three days passed quickly, though the activity was spotty at best. Bondo drove slowly from run to run. They had names like Pyramid, Hemingway, Faux Pyramid (as I used to confuse it with the real Pyramid), and Two Fish/One Rock (which should be self-explanatory and actually once happened). Sometimes we had to cross the river to get the best swing; this was the case at Pyramid. Midway through on one of our crossings, I felt my boots sliding away and was bracing myself for the shock of a forty-degree dunking when I was suddenly swinging above the water; Bondo had caught me by the belt and somehow held me up. I steadied myself and we continued our crossing.

All of that casting, waiting and stepping gave me a good deal of time to consider JD's proposition. I was flattered to be asked, and the position would certainly be a step up from my lowly status as a guide. But I'd grown comfortable with my routine in Belgian Flats. Perhaps too comfortable—despite a set of fairly reliable friends, and a savings account that had edged (barely) into the five figures—a victim of my own inertia. Would it be a further expression of said inertia to decamp to Russia, floating along on the current of least resistance? Probably. But I was always the kind of person who believes that things happen for a reason. Perhaps as JD had phrased it, Russia was indeed calling.

My one fish came shortly after the crossing. I was near the top of the run, a few hundred yards above the eponymous pyramid-shaped rocks, and felt a "pluck-pluck" as the fly, a purple string leech, swung across the current. It *could* have been a trout. But it also could have been "Mr. Steel," as Bondo had taken to calling the fish. I reeled in a few turns of line and took five steps or so upstream and started casting again. After a few casts and a few steps, I was back where I'd had the plucks. "Monkey arms, monkey arms," I murmured to myself. As the fly swung, there was another "pluck-pluck." "I think I've got a player here," I called down to Bondo.

"Then let him play," he called back, arcing a cast well beyond the pyramid rock, almost on to the riprap bank 120 feet away. Not quite understanding his advice, I cast again. As the fly began to swing, it simply stopped. Against all odds, I managed to wait. Do nothing. After what seemed like an hour, the rod jolted and a big fish cleared the water ten yards upstream of where my running line angled downstream. The cold didn't seem to trouble this specimen. It leapt a second time before ripping downstream in a long run that ended in a tailwalk.

"It's Nijinksky!" Bondo cried, hustling up the bank with a large net he'd produced from somewhere inside his waders. I was as surprised at his enthusiasm as his choice of metaphor, given that classical dance had not been central to our previous conversations. If he was able to muster such gusto for each fish that his clients hooked, he was a better guide than I was. In this instance, his delight was not misplaced. The fish took one further run downstream, finding my backing in the process, before coming slowly to the net. Bondo gracefully gathered the fish in the webbing so we could admire our catch without removing it from the water. It was a broad-sided buck with a double stripe—thirty-three and a half inches according to the tape embedded in the net. A good fish anywhere, a great fish for the Ronde. The hook was firmly embedded in the corner of its jaw, but having its barb pinched, came free with a quick flick of Bondo's hemostat. I held the fish by its tail so it could be revived, momentarily overwhelmed by its beauty and my good fortune in finding him.

"He's ready, Cody," Bondo said softly. I released the tail and the fish swam slowly back toward its life. It was the kind of fish that could keep you going for a while.

"We gotta celebrate!" Bondo exclaimed, reaching into his jacket and pulling out a flask.

"Why not!" I replied.

I took a deep swig. Warm Mountain Dew had never tasted so good.

Chapter Eleven

My Life in a Waltz

SOMETIMES I TRY TO THINK OF MY LIFE IN TERMS OF A COUNTRY song. Three chords and the truth, as they say. Or at least three chords and our subjective approximation of a fleeting truism. The four or five months following my trip to the Grande Ronde, passed quickly. Were I to capture them in a waltz in 3/4 time, it would go something like this:

Right after Thanksgiving
The big call went through
With Dmitri the owner
And Quinones too
They asked no tough questions
At least none I heard
They were sold on yours truly
On JD's good word . . .
(Fender Telecaster solo)
Soon Christmas arrived
With a frigid snow squall
I'm not a great shopper
But I went to the mall
Got Mom a jade bracelet
And Dad a new vest
But having me home

Was what they liked the best
The road is so long
But the dream is so near
Keep track of your heartstrings
And don't drink warm beer.
(Pedal steel guitar solo)
I rambled off west
In search of fresh steel
The John Day was so cold
My fingers couldn't feel
So I packed up the truck
With a 10-weight and tent
Aimed due south for Baja
For fish and low rent
The roosters were offshore
At least most of the time
So I sipped cold Tecates
With a small wedge of lime
Made friends with some gringos
Who lived in a cave
Took shine to one sister
My did she misbehave
The road is so long
But the dream is so near
Keep track of your heartstrings
And don't drink warm beer.
(Fiddle solo)
Two months in that sunshine
Left my brains nearly fried
The gringos took acid
And one nearly died
I headed back north
Kissed the sister goodbye
One rooster to hand

Not so great but I tried
Oh the winds they blew cold
As I entered the states
Hit a blizzard near Reno
Had to hole up two days
When I rolled into Baker
Had two weeks to spare
For farewells and packing
'Fore I took to the air.
The road is so long
But the dream is so near
Keep track of your heartstrings
And don't drink warm beer.

Chapter Twelve

Rip Van Winkle

The last few weeks before my departure to Murmansk were a whirlwind of activity. Endless phone calls and a marathon one-day there-and-back trek to Seattle to address a problem with my Russian visa (my middle initial had been registered as "G" instead of "D"); shopping for five and a half months' worth of toiletries and prescriptions for my stay at camp, as well as backup socks and underwear, plus a few pairs of khakis and a blue blazer (some dinners, my liaison Marta at FLIES, the travel company that served as the lodge's exclusive booking agency shared, might be considered more "formal"); lots of quality time with my parents (Mom didn't seem to fully realize that the Iron Curtain had lifted and that going to Russia as an American was not necessarily a death wish); and lots of phone calls and emails to friends from Belgian Flats and beyond alerting them of my coming adventures, but noting that I'd have occasional access to satellite-powered email and to stay in touch.

I reached out to JD on numerous occasions as I prepared to depart, but he was volubly—and uncharacteristically—silent. I didn't even know where he was, let alone whether he had any electronic connectivity to the comrades and acquaintances of his summer world. There were no hard feelings. He'd been kind to me; if he was gone from my life until I next (if ever) touched down in

Belgian Flats, I'd feel fortunate to have known him, and believed I'd gotten the better half of the deal in terms of friendships . . . if one need reduce every human relationship to a transaction.

Marta had couriered me an extensive package of information on the lodge's history, its protocols, blueprints of the electrical grid and kerosene delivery system, fuel shipment timetables, the names and numbers of key state officials and VIP guests, and a sample food ordering sheet. It was overwhelming, to say the least; but I had nine hours on a KLM flight to Amsterdam, the first leg of my travels, and decided to make a dent in the material. One comfort was that the general infrastructure operations of the lodge—cabin and kitchen maintenance, boat maintenance, food ordering and preparation, dealings with Russian officials, etc.—would be dealt with largely by Quinones, the Ecuadorian. My primary role would be to interface with guests, guides, and other staff that came in contact with our guests. "You are not an engineer," Dmitry the owner had said during our call, "and we understand that. You are a person person. And that's what we want." I imagined he'd meant "people person." His English was much better than my Russian, and I didn't try to correct him.

Marta had also suggested that I download WhatsApp to my smartphone. "It's the easiest way to communicate with the people back home," she'd advised. I would probably need a separate app to calculate the time zone differences.

As the plane achieved its cruising altitude over interior British Columbia, I settled into the lodge history. It began with a rather detailed description of the Kola's early human inhabitants:

For some, the Kola Peninsula is also known as Russian Lapland, as it has long been the domain of the indigenous Sámi people, who are known to English speakers as Lapps. The historic Sámi homeland—known as Sápmi—extends across the Kola Peninsula to the northern sections of Norway, Sweden and Finland. Russian explorers from the south referred to the nomadic people as the "Samoyed" reindeer people, the likely derivation for Sámi. Samoyed had various connotations, including Flesh Eaters, Man Eaters and Lone Men.

Archaeological records suggest that humans have inhabited the northern Kola Peninsula as early as the 7th millennium B.C., though it was not until the 3rd millennium B.C. that other portions of the peninsula were explored by people coming from the south. The semi-nomadic Sámi followed their reindeer as they made their way across northern Scandinavia and the Kola, augmenting a deer-centric diet in the summer months with salmon harvested from the mouths of the rivers in the north and east. The Sámi lacked a written language, and relied upon stories that were handed down generation to generation to record their history. They held shamanic beliefs. Though many were converted to Christianity when clergymen arrived on the Kola Peninsula in the 16th century, the new belief system was often blended with the old ways. When the Soviets began to industrialize the Kola, many Sámi were forced onto herding and farming collectives, primarily in and around the village of Lovozero, near the center of the peninsula. Today, it's estimated that less than 2,000 ethnic Sámi reside on the Kola, and less than 3,000 across northern Scandinavia are engaged in reindeer herding on a full-time basis . . .

Before I could get to the settlement of Murmansk—let alone the dissolution of the Soviet Union and the arrival of sport fishing on the peninsula—I was startled by an abrupt bounce. "You slept the entire flight, young man," my seatmate, a white-haired woman with piercing blue eyes, said cheerfully. "I ate your dinner and your breakfast. I hope you don't mind." She grinned beatifically. Even if I'd been hungry, I could not have minded with that smile. Though she was so tiny, it was difficult to picture her eating more than a grape.

After almost nine hours of lodge history–induced stupor, the lights and bustle of Schiphol Airport were disorienting. The machinations of the customs area, which made me think of the turnstiles at a subway station of the future, were confusing. Nor was I clear whether I'd need to retrieve my luggage to head through customs. Marta from FLIES pinged me at that very moment via WhatsApp, informing me that my luggage would be checked through to Helsinki. It must have been five in the morning back at FLIES; Marta, it was evident, ran a tight ship.

My connection to Helsinki was at the far end of Schiphol, but the signage—in bold yellow and black—was extremely clear. (In fact, I came upon a brochure near my departure gate that proclaimed that Schiphol Airport had won a number of prizes for the clarity of its displays.) Midway to my gate I succumbed to hunger, and veered into what looked like a bakery—or would it be a boulangerie? Moving toward the counter with my eyes on the menu, I collided with a young woman who had already secured her order, sending both her croissant and beverage airborne.

"You must be very hungry," she said, a look of annoyance salted with a bit of amusement spreading across her face. It was a very appealing face, I had to say—green eyes, a button nose graced by the smallest hoop and a rosebud mouth, all topped by a short brown bob tinted with a tiny bit of magenta. She was attired in what once might have been called a miniskirt and a crop-top sweater of some soft wool, perhaps cashmere. She wore both well.

"I'm so sorry," I mumbled. "I've been sleeping a long time." She cocked her head, looking quizzical, as if I'd just announced that I was Rip Van Winkle and was desperate to make up for lost time.

"You're American?"

"Yes."

"It's a long flight."

"Especially from the West Coast."

"Seattle?" She brightened. "I am a fan of the grunge."

"I flew from Seattle. But I grew up in Oregon."

"Big trees there. But you don't look like a timberman. I had a café mocha and a croissant with butter and jam. I will secure a seat."

Suddenly I had a breakfast date.

After ordering up our coffee and pastries, Elyse (her name) told me a bit about herself. She'd grown up in Helsinki, but now lived in Paris, where she worked for a large environmental consulting firm as a sustainability expert. Her focus was hotels and other resort-style properties. "I'm aware of the irony—a sustainability person flying around Europe, destroying the ozone layer," she said with a laugh. "But I'm still trying to do my part to help make things a little better." When she asked what had brought me to Amsterdam and I explained I was heading on to Finland and then Russia, she was quizzical. "People travel to Russia to fish? For fun?"

"Yes. And they pay quite handsomely for the privilege. Fifteen thousand dollars is the average price for a week." For no apparent reason, I added, "You fly in by helicopter."

"An amazing thing. When you can buy fish at the fish store."

"We don't keep any of the fish we catch. It's all for sport. But it's very exciting." The furrowing of her brow beneath the bangs of her bob suggested that she failed to understand the thrill of the experience.

"Not very exciting for the fish," she said, nibbling her croissant. "I fly around Europe destroying the planet to save it, your friends torture fish and let them go. We like to think we do our best, but it's all a charade. What a funny world!" She smiled a sad smile that obliterated any bad feelings I had about her harsh stance on catch and release angling.

"Wait," she said, grabbing her phone from a sensible Coach bag and punching at the keyboard. "What is the name of the lodge that you will manage?"

"It's the Pototanga Lodge. On the Pototanga River."

"Well, Mr. Cody. I am looking at my calendar for the summer. And it looks like I am scheduled to visit one Pototanga Lodge the second week in July, to evaluate the potential for a solar energy installation and an improved septic system. I will be, for all purposes and intentions, your employee." Her face became serious. "I hope you will treat me with respect."

I believe I turned white. "As a guest of the lodge and as another human, of course I'll treat you with utmost respect," I stammered.

She burst out laughing, gossamer thin layers of her croissant floating from her mouth, spiraling down to the table. "You look so serious, Mr. Cody. I do not fear you. In fact, I rather like you. But now I must go. To Prague. The Pilsner Urquell facility. A new treatment for their wastewater." She placed her hand on mine and pushed away from the table. "I will see you in July. *Probst!*"

As she blended into the hubbub of Schiphol, I moistened my index finger, retrieved a few of her fallen crumbs and pressed them to my lips. They knew their way around a croissant in Amsterdam, I decided.

Chapter Thirteen

Renost

I HADN'T BEEN ON THE GROUND IN HELSINKI FOR FIVE MINUTES before my phone began blasting. For a moment I thought it was some sort of Finnish greeting—this was the home of Nokia, after all. Though as far as I could tell, they seemed to have lost their mojo. Did they even make smartphones? I couldn't recall having set up my phone to receive international calls. After earning the scowls of several earnest Finns around me—my ringtone was "Stars and Stripes Forever," meant ironically—I was able to fish my phone out of my backpack. It was a WhatsApp call, and the caller had a Wyoming area code.

"Hello?"

"Meet me in front when you get your luggage. I'm in some kind of Finnski sedan, the color red." The voice was unmistakable.

"JD? What are you doing here?"

"Did you think I'd send you behind the Iron Curtain without a proper goodbye? Get the bags."

I stood at the baggage carousel for ten minutes, watching my fellow KLM passengers collect their belongings, hoping that my phone wouldn't blast another bit of unintended American jingoism. There was a tap on my shoulder. A smiling middle-aged woman with long blonde hair parted in the middle stood before me. "You are Mr. Cody? I think there's some bad news about your luggage."

"Really?"

"I am Annelie, FLIES' representative in Helsinki." Before I could mention it, she added, "You might think of me as Marta's Finnish equivalent. Lost luggage on KLM flights coming from America is not an uncommon phenomenon. Thus I am here to act as a facilitator. I suggest that we approach the KLM luggage window."

As we filled out a host of lost luggage forms, I asked Annelie if FLIES was her sole employer. "No," she said, laughing. "That's only on the days when guests come in, and only a few hours. I mostly organize tours around Helsinki for visitors. Touring a reindeer farm is the most popular activity." I recalled the Sámi from the prologue of the Pototanga history.

"What are the odds of my luggage showing up here in Helsinki?" I asked as Annelie walked me toward the arrivals exit.

"I like those odds very much," she said. "At *some* point. Maybe tomorrow, maybe next week. It's always good to have a Plan B in these situations." A car screamed up to the curb, and the passenger window rolled down.

"No luggage, Cody? That happens in this strange and wondrous country. Get in." After a few beats, "Nice to see you Annelie. Has our boy Cody been a problem?"

"Not yet, JD. Not yet," she replied with a smile. Annelie gave me a little peck on each cheek, a nice Continental touch, and I stepped into JD's rental. "I will see you in the morning. Perhaps with your luggage."

I could see some of the taller buildings of Helsinki in the distance, but JD swung the sedan in the opposite direction. "How have you been?" I asked, as it had been almost five months since we'd last spoken.

"The state of being is a mixed bag, Cody, as you must have noted in your great books courses or whatever you studied in the academy. But overall, life has been treating me well." We rode a few kilometers in silence. "I suppose that the traditional send-off for a young man going off to war or some isolated post in the extractive industries might involve a stop at a titty bar, to use the vernacular, and perhaps even the patronage of a house of ill repute, which may very well be legal in Finland, given Scandinavia's more tolerant views vis-à-vis sexual mores. However, in my ongoing commitment to your enlightenment and to providing you with the tools you'll need to excel in your upcoming position, I've selected a different diversion."

Soon we pulled into the parking area for the Nuuksio Reindeer Park. "It is hard to overemphasize the importance of the reindeer for the Sámi people," JD said, carefully selecting a parking space in the far corner of the lot, presumably to avoid any dents or scratches to his rental, though ours was one of the few cars present. "They say that the Inuit people—who the less-informed might call Eskimos—have fifty words for snow. No doubt the Sámi have at least as many words for reindeer. Though if the Sámi language is anything like Finnish, it's a mishmash of incomprehensible consonants that's better left unsaid. I've signed us up for a private tour, which should immerse you in the ways of the *boazu*. The literature says that you will have the opportunity to milk a reindeer and even sample one of the fruits of such labor, namely *renost*, or reindeer cheese."

I found myself longing for the titty bars of Helsinki, whatever shape they might take.

Chapter Fourteen

Murmansk

MY AFTERNOON AND EVENING IN HELSINKI PASSED PLEASANTLY enough. I learned the following:

Reindeer are the primary source of food and clothing for the Sámi people

For a while they were hunted, but then they became domesticated

Renost (reindeer cheese) is milder than you'd think

Alcoholic beverages in Finland are very expensive

I learned the latter as JD, being JD, could not resist what he called "a little toot on the town." And he was adamant that I pick up the tab, insisting that Dmitry, acting through the auspices of FLIES, would reimburse me as part of my travel expenses. I certainly hoped so, as JD's appetite for vodka was nearly insatiable. I stopped trying to keep up with him after the third vodka tonic, opting instead for mineral water or overpriced lagers. The alcohol did not seem to impact him in the least. The only suggestion of a change in his demeanor after two hundred euros worth of Finlandia was a desire to play a few melancholy songs on the jukebox—how Richard Thompson and Elliott Smith had made their way onto a jukebox in a hotel bar in Helsinki, I'll never know. The somber Thompson/Smith vibe seemed well-suited to the Finnish bar demeanor, as most tables were occupied by solitary people who spent most of their time inspecting their drinks and their shoes.

When I arrived at the airport early the next morning, Annelie was there. Her pensive, frowning face suggested that my luggage had not appeared. "Mr. Cody, I am so sorry. I have been speaking to Amsterdam since 4 a.m.; they are *idioottis*. Your baggage is *somewhere* out there," she said, gesturing toward the space between the Netherlands and Helsinki—perhaps Copenhagen. "It will arrive here *sometime*. I would send it off to you immediately, but the helicopter only travels weekly to the camp. And I do not believe that your possessions would fare well in the claws of the baggage handlers of Murmansk. Even with the oversight of Olga, who you might think of as the Russian Marta." Annelie reached into her hefty shoulder bag and plucked out a parcel wrapped in red tissue. My first instinct was that it was more *renost*. "The men working at the camp will have some clothing that they can share until your baggage arrives. In the meantime, you will have these underpants for your private moments." I figured that something was lost in Annelie's on-the-fly translation, but certainly appreciated her thoughtfulness. "They were my son's," she added. Seeing my expression change, she quickly added, "But they are clean."

"Did something happen to your son?" I asked, imagining that I might be stripping a grieving mother of a few last mementos of her child.

"Yes," she said, laughing, though a bit cruelly. "Some Swedish bitch." I would learn later that there was no love lost between Finns and Swedes. Probably something about reindeer. "You will be off now, Mr. Cody," she added, again kissing me on each cheek. "We feel that our beloved Pototanga will be good in your hands." I tucked Annelie's parcel into my backpack and did a quick mental inventory of my luggage, perhaps in a conceptual Copenhagen:

- 1 pair waders
- 1 pair wading shoes
- 2 rods
- 3 reels
- 2 Scandi lines
- 2 Skagit lines
- Many assorted sink tips
- 1 box dry flies
- 1 box wet flies
- 1 nippers
- 1 forceps
- 2 polarized glasses
- 1 fleece hat
- 1 baseball cap
- 4 1x leaders
- 2 spools 1x tippet
- 2 pairs of fleece pants
- 3 pairs of wading socks
- 1 pair fleece gloves
- 1 fleece jacket
- 1 rain jacket
- 3 pairs dress socks
- 3 pairs Levis
- 3 pairs of khakis
- 3 long sleeve shirts (working)
- 3 long sleeve shirts (button-down)
- 7 pairs underwear

- 1 pair hiking boots
- 1 pair loafers
- 1 pair sneakers
- Backups of assorted prescriptions and personal hygiene products

In addition to the underwear of Annelie's son, my backpack held toiletries, a laptop, a pair of shorts and a t-shirt (my sleep-wear for Helsinki), the Pototanga history tome, and a copy of *The Grapes of Wrath*, a little bit of America in its mix of darkness and hope to provide solace should I begin to miss my homeland.

The flight on Finnair was uneventful. One flight attendant sported a bob, and this prompted a reverie about my breakfast friend Elyse, which evolved into a dream—fortunately a chaste one in which we walked along the Pototanga (assuming it was easy to walk along) and I pointed out local flora (of which I knew nothing). If only we could easily assume the skills—and for that matter, the scenarios—that are presented in our dreams. I woke up as the plane dropped below the clouds, and the Murmansk Airport (technically the Emperor Nicholas II Murmansk Airport) spread before me. There were several large structures scattered near the runways. As we taxied toward the terminal—a classic study in the drab, concrete gray architecture that I'd seen on so many PBS documentaries about the fall of communism—it appeared that a few of the structures were tributes to Soviet aeronautical ingenuity. But a number of others were merely defunct and/or partially destroyed planes and helicopters. It seemed an interesting way to greet travelers who had (successfully) landed at Murmansk. I tried to view this display as an insight into Russian character—take joy in the little things that life offers (like not crash landing in Murmansk), as many others have not been so fortunate.

Deplaning in a cold, light mist, part rain part snow, my fellow passengers trudged toward the main arrivals area to the right. I was prepared to follow them when a man in a faded blue uniform blocked my path and pointed to the left. "VIP area for you, Mr. Cody. Please follow me." I followed him into the gray structure, where I was ushered through a series of chutes that would not have been unfamiliar to a steer newly arrived in Kansas City or Chicago. Passage through customs was simplified by my absence of baggage. All of the officials wore the same uniforms as my escort, and the tired faces of a people that had endured great hardship and expected nothing less in the future. I was the only visitor in the VIP processing area.

After processing, I was ushered to the VIP Lounge, which was outfitted like the breakroom in a failing Rust Belt industrial concern, circa 1978. There were a few folding chairs, a heavy metal desk, and a card table that held snacks for the VIP traveler—a few scraps of meat that might have been ham, and a lone dinner roll. The windows on one side of the room looked out on the back of the airport where a few piles of twisted metal (more failed landings?) lay beside a thick copse of spruce. It seemed like a waiting room for one of the lower levels of the Inferno.

Fortunately, my stay was soon interrupted by Olga, the Russian Marta. In contrast to her Murmansk compatriots, Olga was outright jolly. She embraced me like a lost nephew, literally lifting me off the ground. "So you are the Cody?" she said, absolutely beaming. "Marta and Annelie have said so much! I'm glad you are here, the helicopter is waiting. Let us go." Bidding silent adieu to the ham and the dinner roll, I followed her back to the tarmac.

I must say that before my time on the Pototanga, helicopters were an abstraction. I'd seen Forest Service craft circling Baker when forest fires were blazing in the Elkhorn Mountains and had watched Wyoming Fish and Wildlife copters buzz around the Blue while surveying moose populations. Yet I'd never viewed one up close, let alone taken a ride in one. In my mind's eye I'd pictured them as sleek and nimble, like a gyr falcon. The vehicle on the tarmac was more like an emu. The history of the Pototanga that had lulled me to sleep a few days earlier included a back-grounder on the whirlybird in question, mostly culled, I suspect, from Wikipedia:

> If there's a workhorse of the fishing camps of the Kola Penin-sula, it's the Mi-8 twin-turbine helicopter. Without the Mi-8, a camp like Pototanga might not have been possible.
>
> The Mi-8 was the brainchild of the brilliant aerospace engineer Mikhail Leontyevich Mil, founder of what eventually became known as the Mil Moscow Helicopter Plant. It evolved from the Mi-4, a smaller, single-turbine machine. The first prototype was flown in 1961; the Mi-8 entered into large scale production in 1967 for the Soviet Air Force, and has gone on to become the world's most-produced helicopter.
>
> Most commonly used as a transport helicopter, the Mi-8 has a carrying capacity of 4,000 kilograms (either within the cabin or via an external sling). The civilian model of the Mi-8 has also been adapted to convey passengers, conduct search and rescue missions, fight fires and for use as a flying hospital. The Mi-8 has extensive military applications, and is considered the third most common operational military aircraft in the world.

The Mi-8's interior resembled the cargo area of a U-Haul, with the luxurious touch of severe bench seats along the fuselage. Several large prints of the Virgin Mary adorned the entrance to the pilot's cabin, along with rosary beads. There were also several snapshot-size images of what seemed to be lesser saints. One looked strikingly like Elvis Presley.

The pilot and co-pilot were chatting as Olga and I entered the craft and took our seats on the right side. Two men sat opposite, and they nodded at our entrance before returning to their naps. "Those are some of your workers," Olga said as way of introduc-tion. "They will be ready to give you their lives." The center of the cabin was loaded with lumber and several large pieces of iron that might have been turbines. Olga connected her ear protectors and motioned that I should do the same. Soon the great machine roared to life and we slowly lifted from the tarmac. It was mildly disappointing when our vessel veered south, in the opposite direction of the city center. In my mind's eye I'd pictured Murmansk as a kind of Arctic Houston (with less glass), but that picture would have to remain unconfirmed.

CHAPTER FIFTEEN

Pototanga

THOUGH I'D VISITED THE POTOTANGA WEBSITE AND PAGED through its history book (in a *passing* fashion), I was not prepared for the scope of the camp as the helicopter touched down on a swath of cleared land downstream. Most wilderness lodges are a series of tents—bigger tents for the dining/bar area, smaller tents for bathrooms and sleeping. This was no tent camp; it was more a village, carved out from the vast nothingness of taiga and tundra that we'd flown over for two hours en route from Murmansk. There was a wood-framed Quonset hut with a large connected kitchen and a dozen neat, metal-roofed cabins. There was a sauna, a communal showering area (mostly for the staff, as each cabin had its own heated bathroom) and a weight room. There was a boathouse (and a fleet of aluminum craft, each equipped with a jet-propulsion engine), a fully outfitted machine shop (as you can't drive out to Home Depot when you need a few screws), a fully outfitted wood shop, and an office building that included several computers and a satellite internet connection. There was an entire power grid and sewer system secreted under the grounds, which likely gave the Pototanga Lodge a step up on most smaller towns in Russia.

Olga showed me to my new home—a structure I'd share with some of the fishing guides—with private bedrooms and a common area. No one would confuse it with a Grand Hyatt, but it would more than do. I probably wouldn't be spending much time there, anyway. This proved to be very true. "I want to meet you some of the others," Olga said, as I laid my (still) meager belongings on the floor by my bed. I followed her out the door.

"Most of these bozos can speak a little English, but they'll make believe they don't," Olga continued, with affection. "They seem like rough men, but their insides are soft." She introduced me to a few—a blur of Ivans and Sergeys, all thick beards, powerful forearms, and limpid blue eyes. I hoped to project an aura of friendliness and strength, accessibility and confidence. But given the rigors of the previous evening in Helsinki and the bumpy helicopter ride, I was not at my best. My halting hellos suggested constipation more than a shared mission and camaraderie. I took some comfort in knowing that I was not responsible for the oversight of these men who exuded a quiet competence in these surroundings that I could never approximate.

"Cody! Is that you?"

I turned to find a tall and very tan man striding toward me. It could only be Quinones, the Ecuadorian general manager.

"Emmanuel?"

"Yes, yes. It is good that you are here. There is so much to do. And guests will arrive in two weeks."

"That's just 336 hours," I blurted out. Sometimes when I'm anxious, I'll run mathematical equations in my head:

$$7 \times 24 = 168 \ (2) = 336$$

"I hadn't thought of that," he replied. "You are not an operations man, and I understand that. You are a person person. But it's my hope that you'll be willing to assist us with the steps necessary to make the Pototanga a place worthy of princes. We do have princes that stay here, you know. And the chief executives of multinational corporations. They come because we make them feel at home. That feeling is where you come in."

"Of course, I'm happy to assist. Though my bags are still somewhere in Helsinki or Murmansk."

"You will not need your bags to hammer nails and carry large pieces of wood. I can provide you with the clothes of a working-man. I'm happy that you're here."

We shook hands and he turned to walk away. Then he spun around. "We are many of us here into physical fitness, Mr. Cody. Do you like to run?"

"I'm not much of a runner," I had to admit.

"Neither am I," Quinones said, with a laugh. "My activity is parkour." With that he launched himself onto the railing of a nearby cabin, swung onto the rooftop, and flung himself off with a perfect forward flip, landing in the direction of his next task.

CHAPTER SIXTEEN

Making Camp

THE NEXT TWO WEEKS (336 HOURS!) PASSED IN A BLUR. LACKING any specific carpentry, plumbing, or electrical skills, I was kicked from work group to work group, filling in wherever lifting/carrying/holding and any other grunt work was needed. It was refreshing to throw myself into relatively mindless physical labor, especially after the indolence of my past four months. I didn't shrink from any tasks asked of me, not wanting to be labeled a prima donna by my cohorts. I hoped to instill a one for all, all for one ethos. No one commented on my performance one way or the other; I took this as a positive.

I was constantly impressed by the work ethic of the Russians in camp. They worked twelve-, even fourteen-hour days, without ever muttering a complaint. Perhaps it was because they were earning many multiples of what they might be earning doing similar work back in Murmansk or Petropavlovsk, and were grateful for the opportunity. Or perhaps it was a simple acknowledgment that if you take on a job, it has to get done . . . and it's not going to get done on its own. Their ingenuity was likewise inspiring. If they ran short of a particular part while tuning up the jet boat engines or room heaters, someone went into the machine shop and made it. If one of the Polaris quads that were used to cart materials broke down, someone took the vehicle apart and fixed it. Generations of deprivation and closed markets had fostered a steely though quiet independence and resiliency. Some in the American West pride themselves on their pioneer spirit and self-sufficiency. If push came to shove, I'd go with the Russians every time.

The corps of fishing guides—at least the non-Russian individuals—were less diligent in their camp setting-up energies. There was little question that they pictured themselves on a stratified plane in the camp pecking order, and in this self-perception, manual labor was below their station. If the camp were a bull-fighting ring, they were the matadors, the others the picadors, rodeo clowns, and blood sweeper-uppers. True, there were a few famed spey casters and fly tiers in our ranks who'd published books and videos on their specialties—celebrities in our little niche, you could say. But as one of my fellow guides in Belgian Flats once pointed out, being a fly fishing celebrity is like being the world's tallest midget; it is a *thing*, but not a thing that most would care about.

The bottom line was: if you wanted to guide on the Pototanga, you had to help open and close the camp. So the guides grumbled and did as little work as possible. If the Russians were pissed off, they never let it show.

Getting the water turned back on and laying new planks for rotting cabin steps was easy next to the challenges my predecessors faced when the camp first opened. Each structure—mostly canvas tents—had to be assembled, with tent poles fashioned from saplings. Simple bedframes and dressers were hammered together, and stoves were improvised from old engines and mangled aluminum boat frames. Latrines had to be dug, sometimes with dynamite, and outhouses constructed above them. Showers were erected with pulleys to haul warm water up, and cords and cords of wood were felled to heat the tents, cookstoves, and bathing water. The first camp operators were hearty souls; the first guests *really* wanted to catch Atlantic salmon, and were willing to endure small discomforts to do so.

The desire to catch Atlantic salmon seems to run deep in certain cultures, particularly those of the English aristocracy and sundry upper classes. This might be the function of an abundance of free time (like steelhead, Atlantic salmon have been said to be the fish of a thousand casts) and perceived exclusivity (the fish are found in increasingly few rivers, and the land adjoining those rivers—and the rights to fish them—is largely held by those of significant means). Though beyond any sense of elan and broadcasted privilege they might bestow, as sportfish go, Atlantic salmon are a worthy quarry. They feed little or none upon entering their natal rivers, thus must be coaxed or provoked into taking a fly. They're happy to take flies high in the water column and even on the surface. Once hooked, they are capable of long, reel-screaming runs and acrobatic displays. And their streamlined bodies, silver flecked with black spots, are handsome to behold. Having grown up consumed by steelhead, it was not hard to appreciate their appeal.

In an effort to build esprit de corps among the guides and the other camp workers, Quinones lit a bonfire every few nights. I doubt that more than a few would've attended, as the Wi-Fi signal was strong with no guests present to hog bandwidth and most of the men liked to wind down with some internet pornography. Quinones anticipated this and provided an incentive of exactly six ounces of spirits to anyone who'd attend—a choice of vodka or whisky. I presumed he'd arrived at this amount through a scientific inquiry or study of British Naval rum allocations under Admiral Nelson. The great social lubricant did little to encourage conversation, despite Quinones's many efforts at prompts. Some of the men who owned more late-model laptops merely brought them to the fire.

The lodge's few female employees, who would be engaged in cooking and serving guests, steered clear of the bonfire. They recognized the potential downsides of a large assemblage of men in the wilderness fueled with alcohol. There would be a whole summer for them to determine if there were any diamonds among the rough to take home to *mama and nana.*

CHAPTER SEVENTEEN

The Home Pool

WITH THE OPENING OF THE SALMON SEASON CAME THE FIRST
fishing guests, a swarm of leather rod cases, upscale sporting
luggage and unabashed privilege. As JD had forewarned, the
Pototanga's clientele skewed older and decidedly British. Both
made sense. In my experience, it was only older anglers who could
afford to fork over absurd amounts of money for a week of fishing,
and at $15,000 for prime dates, it didn't get much more expensive
than the Pototanga. And with the exception of a certain sub-class
of Wall Street Brahmin, Atlantic salmon were the province of
Brits. Most of their fish in the Scottish Highlands were gone, and
they seemed ever eager to conquer new salmon strongholds—first
Norway, then Iceland, now the Kola Peninsula. Salmon runs may
be the last bastion of the Crown's imperialist ambitions.

The camp's team of guides—twelve strong—plus assorted
kitchen helpers and handymen descended on the heliport to
assist our angling guests with their kit. I positioned myself near
the exit of the Mi-8 to greet our venerable visitors in my role
as camp host, but most ignored me, pushing past to embrace a
favorite guide or other staff member. One man—a Mr. Mac-
Flint—stopped to shake my hand. "You have my gin, I trust?"
he said in a Scots brogue so thick that it recalled a made-up
language from some sci-fi novel. "This Russian vodka is bollocks,"

he added before shuffling along to "his" cabin. Mr. MacFlint, it turned out, had visited the Pototanga on forty-nine previous occasions, making him the most frequent guest in the lodge's history. (There was probably a chapter on him in the history book that I'd overlooked.) A conservative back-of-the-envelope calculation would put his contribution to the Pototanga's coffers at well over $600,000 USD. Cabin One bore a plaque commemorating his many visitations.

He probably deserved a helicopter and jetboat in his name as well.

Though I had practiced and practiced my welcoming remarks, none of the guests paid me any mind. I may as well have been reading the Iowa pork belly futures report. It was obvious they were much more practiced in the routine than I. A few guests immediately decamped for the bar, which occupied the back section of the Quonset hut–style structure that acted as the Pototanga's dining room. Others retired to their cabins to unpack and perhaps nap. A not inconsiderable number of guests quickly changed into their waders and hustled down to the home pool to begin logging their numbers.

The home pool—it should probably be capitalized as THE HOME POOL, given its fame in Atlantic salmon circles—sits slightly upstream of the village infrastructure. Depending on who you speak to, it either begins where the Illipanga, a major tributary, enters the Pototanga, or several hundred yards upstream at a point punctuated by two large boulders that rest in the river.

(I believe it starts at the Illipanga, as the point farther upstream can't be reached by most guests because the water is too deep and swift . . . though it wasn't unknown for one of the burlier Russian guides to carry anglers up to the rocks on their shoulders.) The fecundity of the pool was apparent from my arrival when Declan, a wiry long-time guide who hailed from Donegal, Ireland, brought me down to brief me on pool etiquette. (In retrospect, he was also likely trying to suss out whether I could cast or not. [My waders, rod and remainder of my kit had arrived a week after I set foot in the Pototanga Camp. A small card that read "Sorry!" with a coupon for a box of chocolates was tucked in among my fly boxes.])

"The first duffer starts here," he said, nudging a stone at the edge of the Illipanga with his wading boot. "Cast, two steps. Cast, two steps. If he hooks a fish, he moves downstream so another bloke can step in. If he doesn't, cast, two steps. Cast, two steps. When he's twenty steps downstream, the next duffer can step in. Cast, two steps. Et cetera. Twenty steps, then another. You've got to keep 'em moving. It's a bloody conveyor belt. Go ahead and cast."

I stripped off a few yards of line and dropped my fly in the water before me so I could strip off more line and make a proper cast. As I was lifting the rod tip, the line went peeling through the guides and a fish rolled twenty yards downstream. Then nothing. "You've got to get a little tension on them, you know," Declan said. "Is that how you fish for steelhead?"

"I wasn't quite ready."

"That's overstating the obvious."

I cast the line I'd stripped out, and before it had swung three feet there was a solid grab. Then nothing. "When you feel the weight, set," Declan said, already sounding bored. I pulled off a few more feet of running line and cast again. A fish took as soon as the fly hit the water. I set and the fish cleared the surface. It wasn't a large salmon, maybe seven or eight pounds. But it was fairly bright and accounted for itself well, taking several decent runs and jumping five or six times before I brought it to hand. Declan netted and released it and nodded toward the water, indicating I should cast again. I did so, and before the fly had swung below me, another fish took. It was much like the previous fish. Declan netted and released it again. "I think you've had enough," he said, turning and walking back toward the lodge compound. Four casts—well, three and a half—four fish.

That's more fish than many fishing the Scottish Highlands will find in a season. Perhaps several seasons. That's why people will pay small fortunes for a week of fishing. If hooking an Atlantic salmon—even a smallish one—is the one thing that gets your juices flowing more than anything else, there's no amount of money that seems unreasonable for the thrill of finding fish after fish after fish. (Just ask Mr. MacFlint.)

I later learned that there are several reasons that THE HOME POOL holds so many salmon, especially at the beginning of the season. First, the Illipanga is a major spawning tributary, so it's no surprise that fish will queue up outside its mouth before it's time to spawn. Second, the salmon of the Pototanga exhibit a rather varied and unique life history. Two distinct runs of fish return to the river; a spring run (that tend to be a bit smaller but more numerous) and a fall run (that's smaller in number but larger, fish for fish, in size). The catch is that the spring run fish stay over in the river until the following summer, when they spawn. The fall run fish also stay in the river until the following summer. So come spring, the previous year's spring and fall run fish are joined by the current year's spring fish. That adds up to—well, a lot of salmon.

And the duffers and blokes were soon into them.

Declan and one of the Russian guides, Konstantin, were overseeing the conveyor belt as I made the first of the season's many rounds of THE HOME POOL. One hour post arrival, five anglers were ensconced therein; two were fast to fish, and a third, with Declan's assistance, was releasing what appeared to be handsome hen. (Despite overwintering in the river, the Pototanga fish stayed remarkably bright. Beyond more pep on their first run, new fish were barely distinguishable from their forerunners.) The angler who was releasing his fish, a septuagenarian from Surrey named Jeffrey Dongle, had a clicker attached to his wading belt, the sort of device you might use to track your golf score. As soon as the fish was released, he dutifully depressed his clicker and re-entered the river. Before he cast again, he turned back to the bank. "That's my fourth!" he cried, giddy with his good fortune. "I'm gobsmacked. Last year, Dmitry said he'd comp me a week in the summer if I caught a hundred during this visit. I tell you, I'm going to do it!" He returned to his task. I had little doubt that he would find success.

The fourth angler in the line was finding less satisfaction. Recognizing me as the host he'd hurried past at the helicopter pad, he thrust his rod at Declan who was standing nearby and let me know what he was thinking.

"Do your guides here have any notion of the techniques necessary to ensnare one of these goddamned ocean-going fish?" he barked, spittle flying from his lips. I recalled his name from the dossier of the week's guests that FLIES had forwarded me—a Duncan McCleish, professor of philosophy at Cambridge . . . or was it Oxford? This trip came courtesy of friends and fellows at Cambridge (or Oxford), a thank you for thirty or forty years of "undaunted service" . . . which made it sound as if Dr. McCleish had been billeted on the front lines of some extended military conflict instead of assigning essays on Plato. (Though in these days of culture wars, perhaps it was one in the same.) The look on Declan's face suggested that he was quite ready to bludgeon Dr. McCleish into better spirits with either his rod or a rock. I nodded in the direction of the adjacent angler, and Declan handed me the good doctor's rod and moved upstream.

I debated what to call him—"Dr. McCleish" seemed like overkill (he wasn't performing brain surgery, after all) and Duncan seemed overly familiar, especially to an older Brit. No endearments for English academics (Doc? Prof?) presented themselves, so I went with Mr. "Mr. McCleish, let's see if your fly is a problem."

"An American, I sense from your dialect," he sneered. "As I am the proud holder of a doctorate in philosophy from Great Britain's most esteemed university, I would prefer that you use that honorific henceforth." I should've seen this coming.

"Looks like you've got a Willie Gunn on, *Dr.* McCleish," I said, doing my best to choke down any sarcasm. "With a little copper body to sink it down. That's a very popular fly here. Very good. Let's see your cast." He snatched the rod from my outstretched hands and stepped out into the river. Of course, the fly hardly mattered on a river like the Pototanga—or in any salmon or steelhead scenario. It mattered even less if it fell twenty feet short of where the fish lay. Dr. McCleish had his sink tip and roughly ten feet of line outside the tip of his rod. After some violent thrashing on his part, the line and the Willie Gunn dropped in an impotent bundle upstream. Unless a fish were to become ensnared in the loops of his sink tip, his odds for connecting were low. "Might you feed out a bit more line, Dr. McCleish? I believe the salmon are holding further out."

"I'm not a professional angler, sir," he snapped. "I asked my colleagues who wished to honor my academic contributions to send me to this distant spot as it was advertised as a place where any angler could encounter salmon." He sniffed with what could only be described as impertinence, and added, "Perhaps *you* can *show* me?"

As any guide knows, accepting a client's request to fish their water is a decision rife with bitter consequences. In the best-case scenario, you'll be able to impart a kernel of wisdom or technique to the angler, leading to better angling results in the future. In the medium-bad scenario, your casting and failing to hook a fish might undermine your credibility as a guide—why should I follow *his* instructions if *he* can't catch a fish?

But by far the worst-case scenario presents itself when the guide casts and hooks the fish in question. This serves to insult the angler—"You couldn't catch the fish but I can. What sort of an imbecile are you?!?" (The unintended insult is only worsened if the guide offers to pass the throbbing rod to the client to play the fish in, what an old guiding acquaintance called "the courtesy hand-off.") It also potentially sours the remainder of the outing—what if that was the only good shot you'll have at a fish all day, and now it's been wasted?

I looked to Declan and Konstantin in hope that they could step in and relieve me of my predicament, but both were engaged in netting fish. I took a deep breath and said, "Certainly," though there was anything but certainty in my voice. I stepped in beside Dr. McCleish, who shoved his rod in my direction as if it were something despicable; this was far from the case, as it was a recent vintage Hardy outfitted with a classic Perfect reel. (If this was part of the anniversary package, someone at Cambridge/Oxford had done their homework, and apparently held the good doctor in high esteem.) "With the double spey cast, you can get extra load from the rod—and extra distance—by doing a little curlicue with the rod tip and pausing an extra beat with the tip of the rod tilted back before you begin your forward." I said all this while demonstrating the cast. The reel clicked out a foot or so of line with the force of the cast. I let the fly swing below us, confident that we were still five or ten feet short of where the salmon lay. When the fly had swung to the shoreline, I pulled off a few more feet of line. "Would you like a go?"

"Let me observe the *expert* take a few more casts," he spat. "Expert" may as well have been "cockroach."

I cast again, the Willie Gunn landing five feet beyond the last cast. I was pretty confident the fly was still short of the fish, but coaxed the rod tip toward the shore to make sure it was out of their path. Steelhead were not inclined to take a fly that was jerking along; they liked to see it merely swinging in the current. Atlantic salmon, apparently, were different, as my rod was soon bent double, the reel clicking madly and a bright fish—a recent émigré, in my estimation—was cartwheeling downstream. I passed the rod to Dr. McCleish, expecting him to heap more abuse upon my person. "Good show!" he cried, grabbing the rod. "I've waited for this for twelve years!"

Then the dinner bell rang. The fish tore downstream and then upstream, prompting the other anglers in the queue to reel in to avoid a hopeless tangle and take in the battle. Dr. McCleish fought the fish well, slowly playing it to shore while keeping his rod tip high. Declan passed me his net, and soon the fish was at hand—a sparkling hen, dime bright, somewhere north of ten pounds. The other assembled anglers clapped as I gently removed the Willie Gunn from near the fish's snout—not an ideal hook-up, but it held. When I looked up at the doctor, tears were running down his cheeks. "I can't tell you how I've dreamed of this moment!" he said. I asked Declan to take my phone to take some pictures; a few with Dr. McCleish cradling his fish in the net, then a few of me holding the fish with the doctor by my side. "Grab the fish by the tail and ease her into the current," I said. When she's pulling, let her go." The doctor followed my instructions and soon the fish was free. He turned and embraced me, then called out to his spectators, "Not a bad net man, wouldn't you say? That's the first bloody salmon of my life." This led to another cheer from all assembled. And we adjourned to dinner. Late.

CHAPTER EIGHTEEN

Nostrovia!

DINNERS AT THE POTOTANGA ARE A SET PIECE THAT SEEMED AS important to many repeat guests as the absurd number of fish holding in THE HOME POOL. The ritual starts shortly after the jetboats return from the day's fishing, with a few anglers sidling into the makeshift bar at the south end of the Quonset hut for a vodka tonic or cold lager, some not bothering to shed their waders. By 5:30 or so, crudités begin to emerge from the kitchen—smoked mozzarella and crostini, little reindeer sausages wrapped in puff pastry (a Kola take on "piggies in a blanket"), and, of course, smoked salmon. Other guests begin to totter in, most having showered and some having partaken of the electric-powered guest sauna. (The guides and other staff have their own sauna, a cruder affair fashioned from a toolshed that's fueled by wood and replete with willow branches, should the back or shoulders require a sound thwacking. Each season, several guests venture to the staff sauna for a "real" Russian experience; few return for a second try.)

At seven o'clock sharp the dinner bell tolls, and guests move toward the long table on the east side of the hut. At this point, the guides file in to occupy the table to the west. Since the Pototanga first began receiving guests, guides have been part of the equation, instead of being relegated to the gulag of a "staff dining room" somewhere off the dishwashing area of the kitchen. Yes, they might receive lesser cuts of meat; true, they might be served cod if the paying guests receive snow crab; most certainly, their wine is metered out and consumption monitored (while the grape flows freely for the guests). But the guides—young and not-so-young fishing studs from Murmansk, the aforementioned fly-tying and spey casting wizards from Great Britain, trout bums from the American West looking for a change of scenery, with the odd Argentine or South African whose friend of a friend has some connection to this lodge or that sprinkled in—are encouraged to commingle. Guests may buy their favorite guide(s) a drink or choose to sit at the guide's table for a course or two; guides may slide in next to a guest at the main table during the coffee and desert to trade barbs about missed fish or discuss the following day's adventures.

Given its location above the Arctic Circle, the light tan canvas Quonset hut that hosts breakfast and dinner takes on a romantic glow, especially in the late spring and summer evenings, as the sun slowly sets, but never sets *quite* all the way. Most guests take on a similar glow as the red wine flows (often Argentine, thanks to some connection of Quinones). Every meal is at least four courses—a soup, a salad, a main course, and a desert, and there's no skimping on the quality. The five-person kitchen staff (which includes a pastry chef) works wonders on this forlorn clearing in the tioga, though given the Pototanga's extensive electrical grid, they are able to deploy the latest tools of the culinary trade. The aforementioned snow crab is a perennial guest favorite, though flame-broiled prime rib and reindeer cutlets also rank high.

Whatever the entrée, a standard feature of the Pototanga dinner comes after the main course and before desert, when each guest—or their guide for the day, or perhaps both—stand and recount the most salient aspects of their fishing experience. Most emphasize the huge numbers of salmon they've encountered: ten, twenty, even thirty (especially in the spring). Some will share more personal tales—a luncheon of grilled salmon, a sighting of a gyr-falcon or wild reindeer, a fish that slashed at a fly four or five times without ever committing. Each story is followed by applause, guf-faws, or a combination of each. After the last angler has spoken, the servers—a blend of Svetlanas, Kristinas, and Anyas—pour each guest (and any guides lingering by the guest table) a shot of vodka. This is not the realm of Absolut or Tito's or Grey Goose; the pour is an off-brand, likely unpronounceable distillation from the heart of the motherland. (No one loses here, of course, as all vodka is the same.) With a cry of *Nostrovia!*, the vodka is tossed back . . . or delicately slid among the wine, cocktail, and water glasses accumulated on the table, in hope that its unconsumed contents will not be noticed.

The master of ceremonies for all of this pageantry is the camp host. And thanks to my ultimately successful adventure with Dr. McCleish, I missed a good part of it on my first official night.

CHAPTER NINETEEN

Gentlemen, Start Your Engines

QUINONES WAS NONE TOO HAPPY WITH MY TARDINESS FOR THE opening dinner of the season. His dissatisfaction seemed to express itself in a more frenetic than usual parkour routine as we walked among the docks and the boat maintenance shack.

"You are the host," he said, popping from a piling to the dock surface and back to solid ground. "It is hard to be a host if you are not present." In a flash he was on the roof of the maintenance shack, then back again after an impressive back flip.

I explained the situation with Dr. McCleish, the decision to hold a casting tutorial, and the wonder of his first Atlantic salmon. He nodded. "Dr. McCleish was in the bar very late. You made him a happy man. But from now on, it's your role to be present at dinner. And breakfast. And any other group occasions. The guests will be coming down soon. We'll speak later." He sprang off in the direction of the wood shop, bouncing and bounding off trees and boulders. Basic laws of physics were invalidated in his wake.

The guides were prepping for their first official day on the river. The Pototanga's fleet of Polaris quads were tearing up and down the trail that led from the "village" to the docks, carrying support staff bearing provisions—hearty sandwiches, thermoses of borscht, bottles of red wine and beer and even a few bottles of vodka (for the more alcoholic among our guests). As foodstuffs were hustled into coolers, the guides made last-minute tweaks to their craft, moving anchor ropes, adding seat cushions, topping off fuel tanks. The boats and engines were of American manufacture. The first models sourced from Russia shortly after the dissolution of the Soviet Union had proven to be vastly under-performing. It didn't help that the outboard engines had props, which were prone to busting off upon striking the river's rocky substrate, rocks that were often obscured by the Pototanga's tea-colored waters. Guides were known to carry several extra props in the early days, with not a few angling days ending long after dark, boats chugging ever so slowly upstream to avoid parting ways with their last propeller. (The current generation of Pototanga craft feature jet propulsion engines, which have greatly increased both their reliability and longevity.)

The alarm on my trusty Casio began to gently buzz, a reminder that a few of our guests needed conveyance to the docks. The walk down a gently winding, well-maintained trail is not more than three or four minutes from the compound. But some of our guests are into their late seventies, and the ability to ride from cabin to boat and fish entirely *from* the boat has literally extended their fishing lives. This was likely the case with Mr. MacFlint, the forty-nine-week visitor; it was certainly the case for Maurice LaFlume, another frequent guest (twenty-eight weeks visited), from Paris, who'd lost his right leg to a crocodile while pursuing tigerfish in Tanzania. "It was my fault," he shared one night in perfect English at the bar, where he was perched on his left leg. "I got very hot, and though my guide said to keep my legs in the boat, I didn't listen. At least that lizard didn't get both legs. C'est la vie!" I wish more guests had his attitude.

Messrs. MacFlint and LaFlume were waiting on the steps of their respective cabins. I helped each into the Polaris and attached their rods to the rod holder on top of the quad's cab. They seemed to know each other (I learned later that each had reserved a spot the first week of the season for the past twenty years). MacFlint dominated the conversation on the short ride to the river as we passed other more ambulatory anglers. Lacking French and being unable to interpret MacFlint's brogue, they may as well have been speaking Cantonese. Guides were greeting their sports for the day as I deposited my passengers; who would be fishing with who was determined the night before by Aleksei Levin, the lead guide. Levin also determined which beats were fished. Given the vast swath of the river under the Pototanga Lodge's exclusive control—some fifty miles—one boat was unlikely to see another throughout the day (and certainly not a boat from another lodge, as there were no other lodges). Each angling pair would fish a different beat over the course of the week. Some upstream where they were likely to encounter larger numbers of salmon though fewer fresh fish; some downstream, where overall numbers were lower but there was a better concentration of bright spring-run fish. Most of the beats had huts with a fireplace and ample wood set aside, should guests desire some shelter from the cold rain or snow that can present itself at any almost any time during the fishing season here above the Arctic Circle.

The floating dock was beginning to sink below the river's surface as our anglers waited to board their respective crafts. "Cody, I'm missing one," Aleksei called out, holding his arms up in the universal signal of "What the fuck is going on?" I quickly counted the assembled anglers and Aleksei was indeed correct.

"Wait! Wait!"

I turned around, and there, charging down the path, was Jeffrey Dongle, the angler with the clicker, looking a bit worse for wear.

"I landed a total of thirty-two fish," he panted as he reached my position above the dock. "But I fell asleep along the bank at around five. Has my boat departed? Those rocks are none too comfortable." His face wore streaks of mud, and bits of lichen clung to his hair and shoulders.

"You're just in time, Mr. Dongle," I said, patting him on the back. "That's an impressive night of fishing. I'm sure you can find a breakfast snack in your cooler." He joined the angler he'd been teamed with for the week, an American from Minnesota named Roger Harrison, in a boat captained by Declan. I called for everyone's attention, and launched into another Pototanga set piece.

"Esteemed guests, honored guides. All of us at the Potatonga Lodge are thrilled to celebrate the opening of our twenty-third season. We are all fortunate to partake of the bounties of one of the world's most fecund and illustrious Atlantic salmon rivers." I paused to let the solemnity of this statement sink in. "It is the tradition here on the Pototanga to commemorate this opening day with a slightly special send-off." Natasha and Liisa, two of the season's servers, stepped out from the boat maintenance shed, one bearing a tray of crystal champagne flutes, the other several magnums of Dom Perignon. I popped and poured, and glasses were distributed to guests. "May we raise a toast to the sea, to the river and to the salmon that bring them together!" As guests tipped their flutes, the guides fired up their engines. Glasses were collected by Natasha and Liisa, the engines revved, and the boats bolted out toward the center of the river in a flying V formation, half the boats eventually peeling off to head upriver, half heading down.

In some ways, it reminded me of the beginning of a NASCAR race. With less asphalt, more water, and a sprinkling of birch trees.

CHAPTER TWENTY

Not Quite Santa's Sleigh

My days on the Pototanga settled into a certain routine. Early mornings were consumed with making sure that all of our anglers made it out on the river in a timely fashion. If someone didn't eat pork, I'd have to make sure the kitchen didn't serve that boat ham sandwiches; if a guest didn't get on well with a certain guide, I'd have to make sure that Aleksei didn't put the two of them together. If a guide's drop rope was fraying, I'd have to make sure that Eugeny, who oversaw boat maintenance, supplied a new rope. By 8:30 or 9:00, everyone was off, and I could breathe easier. I'd generally retire to the little office off the guides' quarters to tend to the light administrative duties that were part of my role. If the satellite was in proper alignment with our antennae, I'd try to respond to emails from Marta and her associates at FLIES. They usually concerned a coming guest's dietary restrictions or a request to be teamed up with a certain guide. Missives concerning our supply chain (food, fuel, or parts to keep the sprawling machine that's the Pototanga Lodge churning) generally went to Quinones, who maintained a separate office in his cabin. Though occasionally, we were both copied on communiques from Dmitry, the owner, especially if VIPs were scheduled to visit.

While Quinones managed the actual ordering, I was responsible for tracking inventory. Wednesdays usually found me in the kitchen and bar area, counting bags of oatmeal and sugar, bottles of Malbec and Riesling and lager. I'd also make a pass through the laundry area to check on bleach, detergent, napkins, and toilet paper. (Orders for more perishable items, such as the ingredients for each night's entrees, were committed as "recurring" in Quinones's labyrinthine system of spreadsheets.) The orders were called in or emailed on Thursday and arrived on Saturday with incoming guests. Occasionally it was necessary for a second helicopter, though we tried to avoid it—each Mi-8 round trip from Murmansk cost more than $8,000 USD. Though if such a flight was necessary to maintain the high quality of service that Pototanga guests had become accustomed to, there was no hesitation. Pinching pennies was not part of our manifest.

It was never clear why or how Dmitry underwrote the Pototanga's operations. The guides said he loved to fish and was quite a competent angler. But you didn't need to operate what amounted to a small town two hundred miles from the nearest road to get your casts in. I doubted that it could be for the money. Yes, guests paid close to $15,000 during prime weeks. But given the payroll for forty-odd employees, the cost of bringing in supplies (including fuel for twelve jetboats running six days a week) and the expenses associated with operating an electrical grid and sewage system, my back-of-the-envelope calculations showed the lodge breaking even at best—and that with full occupancy and no free stays for friends and family, which was never the case over a season. One must imagine that Russian tax laws have the equivalent of a write-off. Or perhaps Dmitry simply loved the idea of owning a fishing lodge, something to talk about in the more opulent bistros and bathhouses of Moscow.

He certainly didn't discuss his motives with me.

Regarding *how* Dmitry had made the considerable fortune necessary to dabble with projects like the Pototanga, I preferred not to know. I'd read enough about the unsavory business dealings and extracurricular habits of *some* Russian oligarchs to understand that asking too many questions could prove unhealthy. There were rumors—mostly circulating among guests—of connections to GAZPROM and other unsavory associations. I tried to ignore all this; such concerns were above my pay grade. My salary was direct deposited every two weeks, and my interactions with Quinones and the staff at FLIES (my closest connections to Dmitry) were always respectful and professional.

Perhaps my most important administrative role concerned the collection of staff tips. Each Thursday night, I'd announce that we'd been very honored to have the assembled anglers as guests, that as a representative of the Pototanga Lodge I hoped that the week had lived up to their expectations, etc., etc. Then I reminded the guests that they would need to settle up with me regarding their bar tabs (which were roughly tabulated on paper by the server who happened to be tending bar), gift and gear purchases (of Pototanga shirts/hats/jackets/sink tips/flies), and gratuities . . . preferably in cash. FLIES, in their role as booking agent, provided guests with guidelines for tipping—a daily range for guides, and a weekly range for servers, housekeepers, and other support personnel. It was made clear that tips were pooled and shared equally, according to one's role; if a guest wished to do a little extra for a particular employee, it was suggested that they reach out to that employee privately, and that this gratuity would be in addition to the general gratuities for the week's services.

Generally speaking, our guests were quite generous. If you've already dropped 12 or 15K on a week's fishing trip, what's an extra few hundred dollars to show your appreciation for a job well done, and perhaps help someone who's a lot less fortunate than you? But there were always exceptions. At the conclusion of the third week of the season, an angler from Edinburgh who I'll call Mr. Young (because that's his name) entered my office. "I want to square up with you, Cody," he said.

"I appreciate that, Mr. Young," I said, pulling out the paperwork where his week's purchases had been tabulated. "I have a bar tab of $50 for 10 lagers, and $20 from the fly shop for 4 Ally Shrimps. So we have $70 in purchases, plus your staff gratuities."

"That sounds right, Cody. I think everything's in order." He handed me an envelope that seemed suspiciously thin.

"I'm sure it is, Mr. Young," I replied, nonchalantly sliding the envelope open. It contained 200 pounds. With the pound pegged at roughly $1.50 at the time, I could do the conversion pretty easily. "So, you're leaving $230 in gratuities for the staff?" I added, matter-of-factly. "At the risk of being a nuisance Mr. Young, I have to say that your tip for the staff is a bit light. In our materials, we suggest at least $50 per day for the guides, and $20 a day for the other staff. Did we fall short in some way? Was there an aspect of our service that was less than satisfactory? Because I will address the problem immediately."

"No, no," he stammered. "The service has been quite adequate. Please understand that the envelope does not take into account what I gave to Richie directly. We fished several days, you know."

"I'm glad to hear that everything was *adequate*, Mr. Young. And I hope we'll be able to host you at a future date."

"I hope so too. In fact, I plan on contacting FLIES upon my return to secure a spot for the same week next year. It was smashing."

Later that afternoon, I took Richie Goodwin, our sole Kiwi guide, aside before dinner. "Mr. Lester Young tells me that you had a good few days together."

"That is the case, Cody. He had fifteen fish to hand one afternoon. Five of them on dries." Richie said this with the flat affect that I've come to associate with New Zealanders. At least New Zealand anglers.

"I don't mean to pry, Richie. But did Mr. Young give you any money?"

"Indeed he did, Cody. Slid me a twenty-pound note the afternoon of the fifteen fish. Said it was the finest angling of his life. Is that a problem?"

"Not a problem at all. Thanks, Richie."

Cases like Mr. Young's presented a tricky dilemma. As the lodge's host, it was first and foremost my role to do everything possible to deliver our guests an enjoyable experience. But as the primary liaison between the guests and our staff, it was also important to ensure that our people were treated with proper respect. One very tangible signifier of that respect is an equitable gratuity. By my calculations, he was $150 short of the minimally acceptable tip. My first inclination was a public shaming. This could've been initiated easily enough by alerting a few key staff members and long-standing guests of the situation. But public shaming via a whispering campaign would not be in keeping with the pampering that we pride ourselves on. And Mr. Young couldn't very well be billed for his less-than-generous nature. Tipping is, by its very nature, *optional*.

This was certainly not the first time that a guest had short-changed Pototanga staff on the gratuity front. But FLIES had devised a simple system to avenge those who failed to respect the simple honor system. If a guest failed to tip accordingly, the Pototanga host would inform FLIES staff accordingly, and a small red dot would be placed by their name in the FLIES client database. The next time that client reached out about a choice week on a salmon river or tarpon flat, they would be politely informed that the lodge in question was completely booked, the result of unprecedented demand . . . though in truth, the lodge might have few if any bookings. The client might be offered a much less desirable week, or to be placed on a waiting list that didn't actually exist.

The cancellation of such a penny-pinching guest had no impact whatsoever on the Pototanga's bottom line. There was always a long line of anglers eager to claim a spot during the river's most prolific weeks.

Revenge, as they say, is a dish best served cold.

On afternoons when Quinones was occupied with the circuit breakers of Pototanga's power grid (a favorite diversion of his, and a good distance from THE HOME POOL), I might drop into my waders and visit the river. Technically, a few mid-day casts did not constitute an abdication of my responsibilities; the afternoons were largely my own. But it was an unspoken rule among camp staff that no one should touch THE HOME POOL during the day; that way, it would be fresh for any guests who had the rare day of poor fishing and wanted to get their numbers up, or for those (like Jeffrey Dongle) who simply couldn't get enough. It was wrong to do so, but it was hard to resist the call of so many fish concentrated in such a finite area, especially after so many years of fishing day after day without so much as a bump from the steelhead at home. I justified my actions by fishing a floating line and a skating fly with a single barbless hook. (Double hooks were the rule of the day on the Kola Peninsula, as on most rivers in the United Kingdom.)

No matter how difficult I tried to make the fishing, I hooked salmon every visit. Sometimes the fish took the fly as it skittered across the surface, sometimes on a dead drift. Bombers worked. Bass poppers worked. A Styrofoam peanut (color white) stuck on a bare hook worked. A clear plastic tube on a hook worked. It just didn't matter. The greater challenge was to make sure that I avoided detection. The servers, kitchen and maintenance personnel seldom wandered down to the river, and even if they did, I doubt they would've cared. (Though we never discussed it in great detail, it was my sense that they considered sport fishing a rather foolish and perhaps even childish pursuit. Coming of age in post-glasnost Murmansk, the opportunities for recreation were likely limited.) Quinones certainly would've taken umbrage, but I only fished when he was far from the river. My greatest concern was getting caught out by one of the guides.

Though the Pototanga's outboards had come a long way since the early days, no one would call the current engines quiet. This was a boon to my purposes. Unless the wind was blowing briskly from upstream, downstream boats were not an issue. I'd be able to hear them from a mile away, and would have plenty of time to reel up and scramble into the brush a short back cast from the bank. Even if the wind was wrong, I'd very likely see them before they saw me, given the way the river bends. Upstream guides posed more of a problem. First, there's a long straightaway that begins near THE HOME POOL, providing sight lines upstream for a good mile and a half. The prevailing wind blows from downriver, which muffles even the mosquito-like whine of the outboards. And one of the best runs of the beat directly above THE HOME POOL was less than five hundred yards away. If the guides chose to drift into the last stretch of the beat, they could sneak up on me in near silence. I was always vigilant to scout out the upstream run before stepping in and beginning to cast. But on one occasion I looked up after having rolled a fish three times on a yellow Styrofoam peanut to find Declan and two guests from Finland just a hundred yards above me. Declan doffed his hat before nosing the boat upstream and twisting the throttle.

That night at dinner, after I'd announced the guide pairings and beats for the following day, Declan took me aside. "I see you're patrolling THE HOME POOL, Cody," he said, winking ever so slightly. "Good on you. It's always good to have that in our back pocket after a tough day. It's nice that you're out there keeping it *clean*." He returned to his dessert. The message was clear: *be more careful*.

More often than not, I'd spend my mid-day downtime walking the property, lost in thought. I wish I could say that my ruminations lingered upon loftier topics—world peace, the growing climate crisis, social inequities, etc. Instead, they tended to focus on the more immediate concerns facing yours truly. My ability to perform the duties of my job at the Pototanga Lodge brought me little anxiety after the first two weeks, beyond calming the occasional unruly client and assuaging petty rivalries between overzealous guides. My worries lay further in the future. The internal dialogue went something like this:

CODY: Do you think you'll find yourself here at the Pototanga next season?

CODY: I doubt it. But isn't that a little presumptuous? They haven't even asked you yet.

CODY: Are you going to be a fishing guide for the rest of your life?

CODY: There are less honorable ways to make a living. But you have a point. I have had the good fortune of an education. Perhaps I should do something with it.

CODY: A good education doesn't have to equate with a job. Your liberal arts studies have given you a fuller understanding of life, made you a better citizen and an overall more interesting person.

CODY: Yes. But being a fishing guide isn't really working on a financial level. I mean, I have a little bit of money socked away, but it won't cut it if I ever want to buy a house, let alone have a family. Maybe I need to consider a real job.

CODY: If there's enough love there, you'll find a way. Lots of people raise happy families without ever owning a house.

CODY: I suppose you're right. It's probably just a way of putting off the inevitable.

CODY: What are you talking about? The "inevitable?" You don't even have a girlfriend. You haven't had sex since you were in Baja. And that was, what?

CODY: Four months ago.

CODY: Don't you feel a little . . .

CODY: Horny? Yes.

CODY: What about the servers? Liisa seems friendly. And she's certainly cute.

CODY: I don't think that's a good idea. Camp is a very small place.

CODY: You're the one who brought it up. I'm just saying.

And so on.

It was during one of these long—and to be honest, rather melodramatic—conversations with myself that I met Igor. I had decided to walk up the Illipanga a few miles to see how many fish were holding in its pools; if there was enough water in the river and the fish were present, we would sometimes offer our more mobile anglers the chance to fish a morning or afternoon here. Picking my way along the trail, which had become overgrown from disuse, I came upon a small clearing where several reindeer were happily chomping on the knee-high grass. I quietly stepped back, excited to view wild local fauna in such proximity. (I'd read that reindeer, elk, brown bear, and wolves called the region home, but had not encountered any wildlife around camp beyond the cuckoos that greeted me each morning.) The reindeer were soon joined by an elderly, stoop-backed man dressed in what seemed to be burlap but was probably reindeer skins; he was reminiscent of the English thatcher from the album cover of *Led Zeppelin IV*, though he bore no sticks upon his back. A few other reindeer followed him into the clearing.

Apparently, the reindeer weren't that wild.

"I am Igor!" Igor said. "I am reindeer." He could've been referring to his diet or his occupation. Though recalling the history of the Sámi I'd learned with JD outside Helsinki, they were more or less the same. I explained that I worked at the fishing lodge, and he nodded enthusiastically. "I work lodge too!"

As the reindeer grazed, he went on to share a story. From what I could understand from his telling—and with some clarification from the darker recesses of the Pototanga history book—this is what had happened. Early on, when the camp had first been constructed, Igor had shown up on a snowy day—not uncommon in mid-May—with a sleigh pulled by a few of his reindeer. The season's first guests would not arrive for a few more days. Mitch Fajer, the camp's first general manager, was smitten by Igor and his sleigh, and asked him to come back when the helicopter arrived, thinking the sleigh would be a fun (and efficient) means of transporting luggage from the clearing where the helicopter landed to the center of the camp.

All went as planned. Guests were delighted by the quaint notion of a reindeer-drawn sleigh to carry their bags. Igor was excited too; after all, how many Sámi had had the opportunity to show off their reindeer husbandry to rich Westerners? Perhaps a bit too excited, as he enthusiastically whacked one of his four-legged comrades with an alder branch to get him moving. A stampede ensued. Whether a reaction to the strange metallic bird that had delivered these odd hominids to the taiga or an instinctive response to this sudden and pronounced infringement of capitalism upon the Motherland, the reindeer and the sleigh whipped through the center of the camp and zigzagged through the woods, heading straight toward the river. Fortunately, the runners caught on the exposed roots of some black spruce, tipping the sleigh and snapping the straps that had connected the animals to their payload. The reindeer continued galloping to the river's edge, then stopped abruptly and lowered their heads, as if all they had wanted all along was a sip of water. The visitors' luggage, though scattered among the trees, was undamaged. With the threat of their priceless equipment being swept downstream removed, the assembled party had a good laugh, and all was well.

"They never call me again," Igor said, shrugging his shoulders. He turned back up the trail, his cadre of reindeer close behind.

CHAPTER TWENTY-ONE

VIPs

I AWOKE ONE MORNING TO A LOUD RATTLING ON THE METALLIC roof of my bedroom. My first thought was that a wolverine was initiating an assault. I pulled on some pants and stumbled outside to find Quinones performing a perfect backflip from the eaves of the structure. He followed this with a maneuver that found him running up a wall into another backflip. The pace of his parkour suggested that a crisis was imminent.

"Cody!" he cried. "Did you not see the note? Dmitry is flying in this afternoon. We have to hustle."

I hadn't seen the note as I hadn't been copied on the email, and I wasn't sure what we'd be hustling for. Though we were at the cusp of the slightly quieter summer season (which found fewer fresh fish in the system and slightly fewer guests), the camp was nearly full and things were humming along. I suppose Quinones felt it was important to give the impression of busyness, though in my experience, the surest sign of a well-functioning organization is a lack of rushing about. Nonetheless, I finished dressing and headed into the Quonset hut to inventory our alcohol supply, though this task had been performed three days prior.

As mentioned before, I knew next to nothing about Dmitry Smedryav. I had spoken to him for five minutes on the phone, understood that he was very wealthy, and assumed that he had an interest in salmon fishing, owning a fishing lodge, and/or the general sporting hospitality industry. Of course, I had my preconceptions of an oligarch's habits and trappings. They involved:

- Large golden pendants
- Shirts that were often unbuttoned
- Posses of leather-jacketed thugs
- Penthouses in London, New York, and other cities where ill-gotten gains could be laundered
- A taste for power
- Connections to those in even greater power
- A taste for illicit pleasure

I must admit that I could not have been much further off the mark. Yes, Dmitry Smedryav arrived at the Pototanga in a custom Sikorsky S-92 Executive helicopter (retail price: 16.9 million USD) instead of the dilapidated M-8 that delivered the rest of us. Yes, he had a private cabin set above the river a quarter mile downstream from the boat launch, with its own satellite internet connection, a hot tub, fully equipped kitchen, and sixty-inch plasma screen television with a four-hundred-disc library of DVDs. Yes, he sometimes liked to fish with a Hardy Hotspur Cascapedia reel that was said to have once been owned by Queen Victoria and was acquired at auction for over 100,000 USD.

But for all intents and purposes, he was a pretty regular guy.

I came upon Dmitry the afternoon of his arrival, casting a single-hand rod from the shoreline, not far above the cove that held the boat launch. (He was more observant of the informal rules concerning THE HOME POOL than I had been.) His casting stroke was compact and efficient; with a precise double haul, he easily laid out seventy or eighty feet of line across the water. I had heard the approach of the Sikorsky, but as it was a Friday, I had been busy tabulating the week's bar and tackle shop totals for the week's guests. (It seemed that the buggier early weeks of summer, combined with many fish moving out of THE HOME POOL, correlated to higher alcohol bills for our guests . . . though no formal statistical analyses were performed.) Dmitry was not accompanied by bodyguards or a retinue of any sort. When he saw me downstream, he smiled, waved me up and reeled in his line.

"I finally meet you, Cody," he said, pumping my hand with his right and grasping my forearm with his left. These were strong and calloused hands, hands that had known manual labor, or at least some serious home improvement projects. "I have heard only good things."

"People are very kind. I'm trying my best. But the truth is, it's not a terribly difficult job."

"I don't know. Dealing with John Q. Public takes a calm demeanor and a steady hand. Especially if they are rich and spoiled. For that reason, I prefer numbers."

"Dmitry! Hello!" Quinones came trotting up the path from the boat launch. He was bristling with energy; I was certain it was taking all of his considerable discipline to abstain from scaling and flipping off adjacent trees, as he would feel such behavior unbecoming before Dmitry. "I see you've found our Cody," he said, placing his arm around my shoulders. "He is beloved by our guests and staff alike." This was a bit of an exaggeration, as I was quite certain the camp's craftsmen and a few of the older guides saw me as a weak-willed interloper at best . . . and that some guests sucked up in the hopes that I might slide them into a better beat or knock a few dollars off their bar tabs.

"It's good to hear good things about our camp host," Dmitry said, clapping me on the shoulder.

"Do you have a minute, Dmitry? I'd love to show you the improvements to the electrical grid."

"Of course, of course Emanuel," Dmitry said, attaching his fly to the hook guard on his rod. He winked at me. "Cody? I'm hoping you can take me fishing tomorrow. Will that work?"

"I'd be pleased."

Chapter Twenty-Two

Watch Your Drops

THE NEXT MORNING, DMITRY WAS WAITING AT THE BOAT launch with the other anglers. A few of the guides made it a point to shake his hand and inform their sports that they were in the company of "the founder of this feast." (This was Declan's phrase; a poet seemed to be lurking in his being, a byproduct of his Irish heritage.) But beyond that, Dmitry attracted little attention to himself. He was just another angler anticipating a day of fishing, albeit an angler that owned one of the world's most exclusive fishing lodges.

I had my reservations about guiding Dmitry. For starters, I hadn't put in nearly enough time on the various beats to understand where the fish liked to hold. A week before the first guests arrived, Aleksei spent a couple days showing me six of the most prolific beats, grouped by season: two for the spring, two for the summer and two for the fall, the thinking being that should a guide fall ill or we have unexpected VIP guests (friends of Dmitry's, Murmansk government officials looking for a boondoggle, etc.), I'd be prepared . . . or at least available. Many of the lies on the Pototanga were less than obvious—rock gardens or shelfs that were imperceptible in the tea-colored water. As Aleksei pointed out the most productive section of each beat and the "FG" (Fish Guaranteed) spots, I took notes, using shoreline rocks or oddly shaped trees (if any) to mark the spot. Despite the notes, there was a less than 50 percent chance I'd locate any of the data points that Aleksei shared.

Aleksei also explained the notion of "fishing the drop." The Pototanga is a very wide river. Many of the most promising lies cannot be reached from shore, even by the most gifted casters. And if anglers are fishing side by side, it's almost inevitable that the upstream angler will be covering water that's already been fished; fishing "stale" water is not an experience for which one pays a premium. Fishing the drop gives anglers better access to prime water, without having to share it or even get your feet wet. It works like this: the guide positions the boat mid-river, just above the beginning of the run, and drops the anchor. One angler stands in the back of the boat and fishes to the right; the other stands in the front and casts toward the left. Each angler lets their fly swing until it's below the bow. After several casts (more if a fish swirls and misses the fly), the guide releases six feet or so of anchor rope from a winch-like apparatus, the equivalent of taking two steps downstream. Anglers cast again, and another six feet of rope is released. Some drops might total fifty yards; some over a hundred. When the drop is completed, the guide engages the engine and heads slowly upstream, winding in the anchor rope as he goes. Then the anchor is wrangled into the boat, and the guide motors to the next run.

Fishing the drop certainly maximized our anglers' potential for catching salmon. But it was not without its perils, especially for the guide. Double hook-ups were not infrequent, and two anglers fighting powerful fish in a small boat in a swift river—with an anchor rope thrown in for added drama—was a recipe for chaos. No one had gone overboard yet, though close calls occurred every season as salmon darted under the boat and around the rope with anglers following, hoping to prevent the shattering of their $1,200 Sage and Winston rods. Then there was the task of winding in the rope and retrieving the anchor. Hypothetically, it should be easy enough—the guide starts the engine, turns the boat upstream, puts the engine in forward at a low velocity while retrieving the rope until the anchor is reached. Then the engine is put in neutral, the anchor is hauled in and secured, and you're off. If the drop has been fished in faster water, however, the procedure is more nuanced. The trick is finding the right amount of propulsion to keep the boat moving straight and upstream without going too quickly, thus permitting the guide to keep up with rope retrieval. It's not uncommon for the guide to ask a client—if they seem coordinated and alert—to hold the tiller steady as the rope is retrieved. This often worked out fine; but there was always the client that inadvertently steers the boat over the rope, accelerates too quickly or throws the boat into reverse. On those occasions, the clients would likely find themselves fishing from shore, the drop rope lost or damaged beyond repair, and the anchor lost to the bottom.

As we walked down the gangplank to the dock, I noticed that Dmitry was not alone. A smallish man wearing an overcoat and galoshes in lieu of waders clung to his arm. "Cody! Good morning!" Dmitry called, a broad smile spreading across his face. "My good friend Pyotor is going to join us. He has never seen salmon fishing!" Pyotor looked back at me and nodded before burying his head back into his overcoat. Eugeny had prepared the boat that was reserved for Dmitry whenever he visited; it was identical to the other craft, though was equipped with a fifty horsepower engine (as opposed to the thirty-five horsepower engines on standard-issue craft) and had a special lumbar support on one seat, as Dmitry suffered from back pain. A special lunch had been prepared—I was to grill a few salmon fillets from a fish that had expired in the net before it could be released the day before. (Though the lodge operated a strict catch and release policy for guests, guides and visiting biologists were permitted to take a fish now and again at their discretion.) Aleksei had assigned us a beat called Double Fantasy, which was toward the bottom of the

portion of river that the Pototanga Lodge controlled. His thinking was that this would afford the best opportunity to find the last
of the fresh spring fish and the vanguard of the fall run. According
to Declan, Double Fantasy took its name from an occasion when
a husband and wife angling team simultaneously hooked fresh fall
salmon, both north of twenty-five pounds, while wading one of
the beat's pools, and landed them successfully; after the fish were
released, the couple was said to have—*celebrated*—by privately
adjourning to a sandbar around the bend.

Though, given Declan's fancy for stories, the guide who
named the run may have simply been a fan of John and Yoko.

Dmitry and Pyotor were huddled close together in deep discussion as I opened the throttle and bombed downstream. We had
almost an hour to travel. It was fruitless to engage my passengers
in discussion given the scream of the engine and the pounding
of the river against the boat's aluminum hull. Instead, I focused
on avoiding any rocks that might hamper our progress, and the
overall surroundings. With the Sturm und Drang of maintaining
the happiness of the Pototanga's capricious clientele and the general equanimity of the guide staff, I mostly took for granted the
untrammeled beauty of the river. Pure water, absent of sewer or
industrial runoff of any sort, unimpeded by dams or water diver-
sions, lined by thick forests that had been spared clear-cutting . . .
or any cutting, for that matter. This was indeed the picture of a
healthy salmon river system, a function of its tremendous isola-
tion, and the very deep pockets of Dmitry Smedryav. I couldn't
begin to imagine the machinations that were necessary to put so
much land and river in the Pototanga Lodge's protectorate—brib-
ery? Bullying? Worse? But there was no refuting the result; the
so-called "tragedy of the commons" had been circumvented. No
people equaled many fish.

Sometimes to protect a river, you have to buy it. Or strong-
arm it. Or outright steal it.

Whatever.

We finally arrived at the top of Double Fantasy. I set the anchor for the drop, and it held on the first pass. I must have sighed audibly, as Dmitry turned and smiled. "There is no need for you to have worries, Cody," he said, standing and peeling line from his reel (not the Queen's Hardy, I noted). "We are out to have a day of niceness." Dmitry's little syntactical quirks had a charming, calming effect.

"I appreciate that. Thank you, Dmitry."

Dmitry dropped his fly, a variation of a Bomber, twenty feet from the left side of the boat on a forty-five-degree angle, and let it swing until even with the bow. With each cast, he fed out another five feet of line. His form was immaculate. I reached for one of the spey rods that sat in the rack along the starboard hull. Dmitry must have heard the clattering. He looked over his shoulder and said, "It's okay, Cody. Pyotor will not be fishing. He does not necessarily believe in it." Pyotor shook his head vigorously as a fish rolled and missed Dmitry's Bomber.

"That was a good one," I said, mostly to myself.

"He'll come back. Or he won't. It hardly matters. I'm happy to be here."

Pyotor spoke slowly to Dmitry. "Pyotor would like to share his ideas on fishing. I will translate as best as I can." Dmitry cast to the same spot again, and as his Bomber skittered along, a huge snout broke the surface. This time the hook held, and the fish was soon somersaulting downstream, line spooling off Dmitry's finely machined reel with a steady hum. The salmon's antics did not seem to impact Dmitry one way or another as Pyotor began his discourse. Dmitry's translation went something like this:

"Fish and men live in different spheres. Man on the land, surrounded by air, fish in the water, surrounded by water. Of course, there are times when these preordained roles are reversed, but neither fish nor man survive for long in the other's sphere. I have always believed that these spheres should never entwine. If fish were meant to walk on the land and cavort with men, they would've been born with legs. Or men would have been born with gills and webbed feet. Wouldn't it be odd if this were the case—their paths would still not cross!"

Pyotor found his own observation funny, and laughed a hacking laugh that ended with his grayish complexion taking on a bluish hue. Dmitry's salmon made a brilliant leap at the bottom of the beat, shedding the Bomber in the process. Dmitry began reeling in without comment; Pyotor took a deep breath and continued. Dmitry picked up his translation without missing a beat:

"As humans, we desire to make connections. E. M. Forster. Only connect. The End of Howard. Sometimes we connect for reasons of affection. Sometimes for violence. Sometimes just to mess with someone else's head. Though this is a bad reason for connecting. That to me is this fishing for sport. You're fucking with their head. And probably their lips. It's a bad business."

With that, Pyotor became quiet and looked downstream, perhaps expecting E. M. Forster or one of his descendants to come chugging up the river. I'm fairly sure that I'd read *Howard's End* when I was in Missoula, though its plot was escaping me. I don't think it involved fishing.

"Should we drop, Cody?" Dmitry asked, though not with impatience. I released six feet of rope, we slid a few yards downstream and Dmitry began casting again. Pyotor seemed to have fallen asleep. Within three casts, Dmitry was fast to another salmon. His face didn't betray any excitement, though the slightest smile spread across his lips.

It's nice to own a healthy salmon river.

CHAPTER TWENTY-THREE

Elyse

THE REMAINDER OF DMITRY'S VISIT WENT SMOOTHLY. I TOOK him out for one more day's fishing on the Pototanga, and he invited me to join him in his private helicopter to fly into a river that held whitefish in good numbers. I was amused as to why someone would spend thousands of dollars in fuel to *intentionally* cast to whitefish, but a chance to fly in Dmitry's sleek Eurocopter was too much to resist. Zipping up and down the river valleys felt like being part of a video game. Though of course, that's a dumb description, as someone must have zipped around in a real helicopter/rocket/jet *before* someone thought to put it in a video game.

Pyotor did not accompany us. The last night of their stay, I realized why—he'd been holed up in Dmitry's cabin, practicing some new compositions on his balalaika, which he debuted for the camp. The instrument has only three strings, but I must say that Pyotor made each of them sing. The Russians seemed to especially enjoy his performance, and several joined Quinones in a spirited dance that resembled an exercise routine and spilled from the dining room into the central clearing.

With Dmitry's departure came the beginning of the summer doldrums. This was the time of few if any fresh salmon, when present salmon's silvery patinas diminished toward brown, and of greatly discounted fishing packages . . . and bugs. Many bugs, both mosquitoes and black flies. The walks around the camp that proved so satisfying a month before were no longer in the equation, unless a brisk breeze was blowing. Guests and non-Russian workers limited their outside time to scurrying from their cabins to the dining room or boat launch; the Russians didn't seem to care. They'd endured so many hardships, a mass of biting bugs barely registered.

One Friday, as I was tallying the week's gear and beverage invoices for current guests and reviewing the manifest for the coming week's arrivals, I came upon the name Elyse Makinen, an agent of Greenwater Consulting. Elyse! My fleeting friend from the Amsterdam airport. It would be a lie to say that I had not thought of her since our meeting several months before. Though a few of our servers—and one or two of the younger wives of some of our long-time clients—were certainly attractive and perhaps available (if only thanks to a perceived notion of my power in the organization), none had the verve of Elyse, with her brown bob, button nose, and sense of irony. If I were to approach her in a more than professional way, it would have to be with the utmost decorum. It would be beastly of me to come on too strong; after all, she was a woman in a remote place with no clear recourse to overly aggressive overtures. And I was the client-facing representative of an esteemed lodge.

Of course, it was quite possible that she had a boyfriend. Or a girlfriend. Or neither, but a less-than-zero interest in me.

I decided I would play it cool.

But that Saturday morning as the Mi-8 created a miniature tornado above camp, I was clutching a cardboard sign that read *Elyse Makinen* in bold magic marker. After shyly smiling pensioners who'd likely saved for years to afford a discounted week on the Pototanga (the sort of guests I especially wanted to please) and a foursome of City of London types (who'd likely come to drink and try to bed one or all of the servers), Elyse stepped off the helicopter. She was wearing tan jodhpurs, a safari shirt with a photographer's vest, an olive Tilley hat, and brand-new hiking boots—the picture of a Parisienne's idea of what you might wear to a remote Russian fishing camp.

"Where should I pick up my luggage, chauffeur?" she purred, placing her arms lightly around my neck and giving me a double cheek European-style kiss. I had not expected such a greeting, and I blushed a brilliant red. Aleksei yelled something in Russian, and the other Russians laughed. Elyse looked to me for clarification. I had picked up enough slang during my brief tenure to understand that they had said something along the lines of "Mister Cody's got a hard-on!" I told her it was an inside joke among the guides.

As we walked the trail that led to the camp, me carrying one of Elyse's bags and she the other, a familiar voice boomed out from the landing pad downstream. "Goddamn, boy! Ain't you gonna carry my bags, Cody?"

I now knew the identity of the last guest on the manifest, who'd been listed as TBD.

CHAPTER TWENTY-FOUR

Elyse . . . and JD

THE VOICE WAS UNEQUIVOCALLY THAT OF ONE JD SMITHERS. While his appearance on the Pototanga was a surprise, in retrospect, there had been some foreshadowing of his travels in the cryptic texts and emails he'd posted. One had read: "How's it going? Oughta see for myself!"; another, "You head far enough west, you start heading east." It was unclear whether he'd been sent by someone at FLIES to check in on me, been offered the slot of a guest who'd had to cancel at the last second, or ponied up his own six grand (plus flights and gratuities) to visit the camp. It didn't really matter. He was here, and would not likely prove an asset in my effort to win the heart of the young and beautiful Elyse.

That night at dinner I was seated at the head of the table, as is custom for the camp host. Elyse was seated to my right, flanked on her right by Quinones, who was championing the greening of the lodge. JD was on my left. As I was trying to parse Elyse's responses to Quinones's rapid-fire questions, JD all but drowned her out, recounting the season in progress on the Blue at the volume of a bullhorn.

"I had a set of twins in my boat in the heat of the cicada hatch. They were both left-handed, and they insisted on sitting

in front. Did I mention they were both named Bo? B-O and
B-E-A-U . . ."

Normally I would've found JD's stories engaging, but now
it was unwelcome white noise. I excused myself, stood up and
tapped a wine glass with my butter knife as Natasha and Liisa
set out bowls of borscht before our guests. "On behalf of Dmitry Smedryav and the staff of the Pototanga Lodge, I'd like to
welcome you all. I'm confident that a special week of fishing and
camaraderie here at a very special spot carved lovingly from the
wild taiga awaits you." Admittedly, I was laying it on a bit thicker
than usual.

"We have a special guest with us this week, Elyse Makinen," I
continued, pointing to Elyse. "Elyse will not be fishing but will be
helping us explore the possibility of adopting solar power to help
fuel our operations . . ."

"To the green revolution!" Quinones cried, standing and raising his glass with the fervor of Che Guevara upon his arrival in
Havana. A toast was drunk. JD had begun coughing; I thought
that a crouton had gone down the wrong pipe and was trying to
recall the Heimlich when he shot me a dirty glance. "I'd also like
you to welcome JD Smithers, a celebrated guide from the United
States, and . . . ah . . ."

"The new minority owner of the Pototanga Lodge," JD
boomed. "Though of course I mean minority in the context of the
proportion of ownership, not in reference to my ethnicity, skin
color, sexual orientation, etc." Everyone sipped from their drink. I
nearly dropped my glass.

As bowls of borscht—some full, some consumed—were
cleared away, I sought to regain my composure. JD was an owner
of the Pototanga? Where had he found the money? Had he
always had the money, and was it just hidden? As usual, he anticipated my thinking.

"Dmitry needed a large favor, and I was in a position to help,"
JD said sotto voce, though anyone on our side of the long table

could have heard. "I have no financial stake in the operation, per se. More an open door to visit the lodge at my discretion, and a certain say in big-picture management decisions, such as key personnel and operational infrastructure." At the latter utterance, he looked at me and then Elyse, raising his eyebrows in a cartoonish fashion. He could lay it on thick too.

"I hope I can make a convincing case for the sun," Elyse said, smiling and lightly touching JD's hand across the table.

"I am very open to new ideas," JD said softly, winking at me.

Chapter Twenty-Five

My Jealous Fantasies

AFTER DINNER, I MADE THE ROUNDS OF THE CENTRAL REGION OF the camp to make sure everything was ship-shape, and then returned to my room in the guide enclave to stew in jealousy. I wasn't particularly thrilled to have JD in camp (an owner, no less!), and was even less enthusiastic to see him flirting with Elyse, who I realized I was attracted to in more than a passing way.

I began to wonder if I was sliding into a routine I'd experienced all too frequently before:

1. Cody meets a nice woman

2. Cody befriends nice woman

3. Cody fails to notice woman's interest in him and/or express his own

4. Cody does nothing to advance friendship to romantic relationship

5. Woman takes up with some other bastard, and Cody is out of luck

Two courses of action presented themselves:

1. Make my case to Elyse

2. Discredit or otherwise undermine any overtures on JD's part

Coming on too strong to Elyse seemed like a poor idea, given my role as her host and erstwhile protector. So I contemplated how I might torpedo JD's reputation. The challenge was, beyond his casual guiding on the Blue, I knew nothing of his background and little of his character (aside from a propensity for heavy drinking and bombastic rhetoric). And I couldn't even confirm that he had any intentions for Elyse beyond a need to be the center of attention. Slandering him on social media would have no impact here. And dumping a bunch of vodka bottles outside of his cabin door seemed childish, and might only enhance his allure.

In the end, I opted to simply retire to my lonely cot and fume about what I might have done. (See step 4 above.)

Chapter Twenty-Six

The Greening of the Pototanga

PARKOUR MAY HAVE BEEN QUINONES'S SPORTING PASSION, BUT sustainable development was his professional focus. Hardly a conversation could pass without him alluding to "greening initiatives." For example:

> ME: Should I have Raskolnikov bring more water down to the boat dock?
>
> QUINONES: We should really explore the use of water jugs and reusable cups. Do you know how many millions of tons of plastic are floating in the Pacific?

Or

> ME: The employee bathrooms are getting low on toilet paper. Should I put an order in for the next delivery, or might we have some stashed away somewhere?
>
> QUINONES: A number of tests show that earthworms can consume ten times their weight in human waste—a week! And their resulting compost-like excrement can be used to fertilize crops.

His intentions were certainly noble, in a think globally/act locally kind of way. Though it was hard to reconcile Quinones's modest enterprises with the belching Mi-8s flying into camp several days a week to deliver every ounce of supplies the camp required, each consuming some 225 gallons of fuel for every hour in the air. And the barrels and barrels of petrol consumed by the jetboats. And the kerosene burned to run the generators that kept the lights on and provided heat and hot water.

It was an uphill climb. But you have to start somewhere.

That somewhere happened to be the door of my room, which Quinones was vigorously knocking upon early the morning after Elyse and JD's arrival. "We need to make the most of Ms. Makinen's visit, Cody!" he cried as I cracked the door open. "Join our tour of the facilities." I'd hoped to shower or at least brush my teeth before meeting Elyse on her first full day in camp, but progress cannot stand still. I pulled on some jeans and a sweatshirt, and nearly bowled Elyse over, as she was sitting on the steps of the cabin I shared with the guides.

"Moving fast and breaking things," she said with a smile. "Just like the Facebook."

Quinones was in his element as he explained the bowels of the Pototanga infrastructure. (That he once again resisted launching into some parkour routine as he explained the generator footprint was testament to his professionalism and the gravitas with which he treated his role as general manager of the Pototanga Lodge.) Elyse listened patiently, occasionally asking a question and making notes on a little tablet computer. When Quinones dug especially deep into one operational minutiae or another, she'd glance over at me and squint her eyes. Or maybe it was a wink. It left me flustered.

JD did not participate in our greening tour, despite his enthusiasm of the previous evening. Perhaps he was wading THE HOME POOL.

At the conclusion of the tour, Elyse asked Quinones if she might be taken out on the river to better understand the lodge's use of the jetboats. "I'd love to, but I need to join a call soon. Let's arrange a time for tomorrow."

"Perhaps Mr. Cody could take me?"

Chapter Twenty-Seven

The Tunnel of Love

From when I was a child—or at least a child old enough to have a romantic interest in girls—I'd fantasized about the Tunnel of Love. The idea of floating into a dark space with a girl I cared about and—what? Holding hands? Stealing a kiss?—tantalized me. I wish the notion had been inspired by the fine Dire Straits song of the same name, but it was more likely the Disney ride "Pirates of the Caribbean," which in my memory involved a boat and darkness. Whatever the case, the idea of piloting Elyse around the Pototanga rekindled my Tunnel of Love reveries.

Now it might finally come to pass, minus the darkness.

I offered her my hand to help her step into the boat, but she jumped in with both feet forward, landing with the poise of a gymnast. "I was on the balance beam as a girl," she said with a smile, taking a middle seat. "Show me the wonders of this salmon paradise."

I took my stance by the engine tiller and off we went. I began to explain how the lodge had shifted from two-stroke to four-stroke engines to cut down on emissions, and that we encouraged the guides to not run them at full throttle to conserve fuel. She waved her hand. "I appreciate this, Cody. But I don't really care. I want to see the river. Maybe catch a fish. And learn more about why people would come here. And about you, of course."

I tightened my grip on the tiller.

In truth, I was much more comfortable giving Elyse a river tour than a sustainability tour, as I'd already more or less exhausted my knowledge on that topic. Though the river was not fishing at its best given the time of year, there were a few runs that seemed to always hold salmon. One was a run called Knock Knock (so named for two hard-drinking brothers who were staggering around the boat while fishing there many years ago, "knocking about" in the words of their British guide). It was not on the angler rota this day, so we roared downstream. It was hard to converse over the four-stroke, but Elyse's smile as she tilted her head back and closed her eyes spoke volumes. I cut the engine and we drifted into the top of Knock Knock. I dropped the anchor to set up the drop.

"Now what, Mr. Cody?"

"Now we fish. Or you fish." Most of our clients fished spey rods, and we always kept one or two in the boats should a client's outfit break or otherwise malfunction. Picking one up, I explained that the fly itself had little to no weight, and thus it was the fly line that had the mass needed to initiate a cast; that the spey cast was the preferred methodology for covering large pieces of water on a large river like the Pototanga as opposed to the traditional overhead cast, which she might have seen in the movie version of *A River Runs Through It*; that the "D-loop" was an essential element of the cast, and that it was important to keep the loop to the right of your right shoulder (or the left of your left) when casting off that shoulder, lest you send the fly speeding toward your scalp; that the forward motion of the rod to initiate the cast was more akin to flicking a pea with a spoon (perhaps at your younger brother or sister) than a slow sweep to the water. Then I stepped into the casting station at the left front of the boat, stripped off 30 feet of line and demonstrated a cast. I was sure to re-cast before the fly had swung below us, as many takes occur on the dangle. "Do you see the D-loop?" I asked.

"D for delightful," she said dreamily. "Though it really appears more like a C."

"Would you like to try?"

"Of course." I'd hoped that she'd find it an awkward motion and would need me to stand behind her and mimic the casting motion, in effect throwing herself into my arms. But she took the rod and easily laid out the thirty-odd feet of line, the reel bucking, wanting to release more line. She understood this and peeled off more line, casting forty and then fifty feet. "This is a very pleasing motion, Cody, even without the fish," she said.

"If you let the fly swing to below the boat, you might even catch one. If you feel a tug, don't do anything until you feel the weight of the fish, then swing the rod to your right side." It wasn't until the third drop, but a fish was waiting. Elyse let the fish turn and then smoothly set the hook. She must have found an early fall fish, because it was off to the races in a flash, cartwheeling and somersaulting downstream. I hadn't warned Elyse about the possibility of having her knuckles rapped by a spinning reel handle, as it seemed more likely that she'd encounter a holdover fish from this spring or last fall, one with less zip. But this wasn't the case. She let out a little cry—more like a groan—and dropped the rod. It clattered on the floor, line still zipping off. "Please sit down," I said, while casually picking up the rod. I clamped the drag down and the fish slowed. "Let me see your hand," I said, holding the rod high to keep tension on the fish. She held it out tentatively, and I took it in mine. The reel handle had skinned the knuckles on her index and middle fingers, but otherwise she was okay. When I released her hand, I glanced up. She *may* have been blushing.

"I'll get the first-aid kit," I said, stepping around her while keeping the rod high. The fish was splashing far downstream, but seemed firmly hooked. "Would you like to hold the rod for a second?"

"That fish does not seem to care for me. So thank you, no."

I managed to dislodge the first-aid kit (each boat carried one) from beneath one of the seats and suggested that Elyse apply some antibiotic cream to her knuckles. I longed to do so myself, but the salmon seemed to have other ideas, now reversing course and screaming toward the boat. The fish had become a bit of a white whale for me, and landing it presented an opportunity to show Elyse my affection and allegiance; it had hurt her knuckles, and now it would pay. I reeled like mad to close the gap, then tightened the drag down further. A few good pumps of the rod brought the fish closer; it would be ready for the net soon. I snuck a glance at Elyse, and she did not look impressed. In fact, she had produced the tablet computer from her purse and was typing. Deflated, I muscled the fish to the boat. It was a beautiful specimen, nickel bright, just north of fifteen pounds.

"Would you like to see it?"

"What's that? Oh, sure." Her enthusiasm rivaled that of someone asked to view a friend's latest cat video. She stepped to my side of the boat. "To think they've swum so far," she murmured. She reached down tentatively to stroke the fish that lay serenely in the net. I popped out the hook, grabbed the fish around the tail and held it in the current. Soon it wriggled, signaling its readiness to go. I opened my hand and off it swam.

"Would you like to see more of the river?" I asked.

"I'm happy to rest here for a moment," she replied. "We'll save fuel," she added, with the slightest smirk.

"As you wish."

I buttoned up the spey rod and tucked it back in its place below the right gunwale. Then I fiddled about with the first-aid kit for a bit, though it didn't require any reorganizing. After the brush of our fingers, I was more than a little deflated by the salmon's anticlimactic landing. Instead of being a hero, I was a one-dimensional egotist eager to show off. Elyse proved most empathetic.

"The fish was very pretty, Cody. It was very pleasing to feel the pull of its power. But I suppose that was enough for me. But you like fishing. And that's okay. Everyone has their passion."

I couldn't help but smile. "What are your passions, Elyse?"

"It is kind of you to ask," she said, closing the cover of her tablet. "My work is very important to me. I know it can seem—what do you say—a fool's errand? The Pototanga shifts to solar energy. Maybe you burn 10,000 or 20,000 fewer gallons of kerosene. But China adds 15 million new cars each month. Whatever I do is a drop in the bucket. But we have to try. I also am very interested in sex . . ."

My mouth must have dropped, as Elyse quickly added, "On a theoretical level. I am Scandinavian, after all. What brings our bodies together? A desire for intimacy? For pleasure? A biological imperative? An act of subjugation? Of fetishism? A quest for power? It's an interesting topic, and I'm an avid reader. Though I'm not averse to experiential research." At this, she raised her eyebrows ever so slightly.

Before I could respond, the boat's radio began bleeping, and there was the unmistakable voice of JD Smithers. It was muffled as if he were speaking into the wrong side of the receiver. "I can't quite hear you, JD," I said into my receiver. After a few muted expletives, he must have turned the receiver around. "Cody?"

"Yes, this is me."

"Is Elyse with you?"

"Yes."

"That's nice. She's quite a young lady. Hi Elyse!"

"Hi, JD," she called, though I'm not sure the radio picked her up.

"Cody. There's a situation here. It's a little difficult to explain. Can you motor back?"

"We'll come right away, JD."

"Bring Elyse."

"She's in the boat with me."

"Good."

With Elyse working the tiller, we made quick work of retrieving the anchor. A front was coming through, and the temperature had dropped. She asked if she could sit by me. "For warmth," she added.

I didn't object. Her shoulder brushing against my hip was enough to cushion me against any problems that awaited us at camp.

CHAPTER TWENTY-EIGHT

Where's Quinones?

THE NEWS THAT QUINONES WAS NOWHERE TO BE FOUND WOULD normally not be a cause for concern. If things were running smoothly—and they usually were—it was not uncommon for him to disappear for several days into the taiga with only a gallon of water, part of an effort to reduce his body fat to less than 6 percent. He would also sometimes fly back to Murmansk on the Mi-8 after mid-week supply deliveries, as the functioning of supply chains fascinated him almost as much as green engineering systems and parkour. But given Elyse's presence, and his eagerness to move forward on the solar power initiative, it made no sense that he'd go AWOL.

JD was waiting at the dock as we pulled in, clutching a can of Sierra Nevada pale ale. "You may want one of these," he said, pulling another Sierra from a pouch in his jacket. "It seems we've had an abduction. Quinones is gone." I began to explain his proclivity for occasional forays off campus, but JD cut me off. "There is a note. Here." He passed me a flyer that we passed out to guests showing the proper way to release a salmon. On the back, a message was scratched out in florid cursive:

Quinones is gone

That's plain to see

He won't be back

'Til you free Z'ablee

The doggerel was decorated with a stick figure drawing of a man—presumably Quinones—hanging from a railing. It might have been an execution, or a nod to his acrobatics.

"What's this Z'ablee business?" JD asked.

Z'ablee was a beat near the bottom of the Pototanga, just above tidewater and the southernmost of Dmitry Smedryav's holdings. Though it was close to the ocean, it wasn't considered a particularly productive beat. The river was wide and shallow through most of Z'ablee's length, and there was little in the way of structure. Fish tended to blast right through, though if you caught it as pods were arriving, the fishing could be excellent. Considering the long run from the camp—nearly one and a half hours each way—it was the Pototanga's "risk/reward" beat. Beyond the first few weeks of the spring season and late August/early September, we didn't send clients there. If fresh fish weren't moving in, there was no sense. I also knew (from the Pototanga history tome, which I did *eventually* read) that the lands adjoining the Z'ablee beat were very special to the Sámi people. The researcher's translation of the Russian historical text was a bit unclear, but it seemed to suggest that the region's importance stemmed from the easy crossing it afforded the Sámi's reindeer, or was a place where they'd take the reindeer for recreational swimming.

"I think the Sámi want their land back," I said.

"They are not, I think, a warlike people," Elyse offered.

"How would you know?" JD asked in a rather dismissive tone.

"We have Sámi people in Finland. Can I have a beer, please?" JD produced another from somewhere in his coat. I remembered Igor, the reindeer herder that I'd run into on the Illipanga earlier in the season. Could there have been a connection?

"I think we should get Dmitry on a call," I said, ushering JD and Elyse into my little office. I had not had occasion to call Dmitry—this was Quinones's domain—but numbers for his various offices were alphabetically arranged on a long Post-it note stuck to the side of my computer monitor. A few—London, Brussels, New York—were obvious business centers. But others—like Akureyri, Iceland; Fredericton, New Brunswick; and Alta, Norway—suggested proximity to other Atlantic salmon rivers. Each of the offices was staffed by a live operator, twenty-four hours a day, seven days a week. After three calls, we were able to locate him in New Brunswick, where it was morning. (Dmitry no doubt had a cell phone set aside for emergency situations like this, but Quinones would never share that number. It was a source of power.)

After a long pause, the operator patched me through. "Cody, I am glad to hear from you. But there is a problem?" The splashing of a river could be heard in the background, along with the sound of line being pulled from a Hardy Perfect reel.

"Quinones is gone," I said, as calmy as I could. "There was a note tacked to the door of his cabin. A kind of ransom request."

"Is that so?" Dmitry said. Laughter could now be heard, and some conversation, perhaps in Quebecois. I could make out the word "Bomber." JD was waving his hands in the air like he had something important to say.

"JD wants to speak to you," I said, handing him the phone.

"Dmitry? Hello! I'm here at camp," JD said. "How's the Miramichi treating you?"

"Good. May I speak to Cody?"

"Of course."

"Cody. What did the note say?" I recited it verbatim. And I mentioned that I'd run into Igor near camp earlier in the season. "I have had discussions with Igor and the Sámi before. I have tried to make it clear that they are welcome to camp on the land and use the river. My lease merely gives us the right to fish with flies. And the authority to prohibit others from fishing. Poachers would come from Karelia and stretch gill nets across the river. Imagine the carnage! But the Sámi are not well-versed in contractual language, though this is not to say they are unintelligent. They believe in actions before words. Who can blame them, after the way our governments have taken their land."

"How should we proceed?"

"The Sámi are not a vengeful or violent people," Dmitry continued. Elyse glared at JD, who looked out the window as though he were no longer listening. "I imagine that Quinones is in good hands. They may have traveled by reindeer, or they may have hidden a boat below camp. But it would be my guess that you will find him with Igor and his men on the banks of Z'ablee by tomorrow afternoon." There was a pause. "Is the green woman there, Cody?"

"The green woman? Yes, Elyse is here."

"I suggest you bring Ms. Elyse as your companion. The presence of a woman will signal that you come in peace."

"I know a bit of the Sámi language," Elyse added.

"That cannot hurt," Dmitry said. "JD, you stay at camp and watch over things." The scream of a Hardy could be heard in the background with some excited hollering. "Cody, you have my authority to cede the Pototanga Lodge's right to fish the Z'ablee beat. You can tell Igor that he has my word, and that I will deliver my right thumb should I not honor that word. He will understand. We will continue to defend the water from poachers, of course. That's in everyone's best interest.

"I have to go now. Please call once you learn more."

CHAPTER TWENTY-NINE

Twice Caught?

THAT EVENING AT DINNER, I MADE NO MENTION OF QUINONES'S disappearance. One guest (who apparently shared an interest in solar power, supply chains, or parkour) asked about his absence, and I said he was feeling a little under the weather and resting up in his cabin. That seemed to satisfy the guest's curiosity. I noticed a lot of whispering at the guide table. I caught their attention and ran my index finger across my throat, the sign for *cut it out*. I forgot, of course, that our guide corps was international in scope, and my sign might not be as universal as intended. Several guides began to mime, placing imaginary guns against their heads and pulling the trigger, or nooses around their necks and tilting them at a grotesque angle. I shook my head and returned to my master of ceremonies' role.

It came time to recount each boat's catch of the day. I liked to wait until after the main dinner course for this bit of pageantry, as some guests could go on at length about their river escapades, and I hated to see entrees go cold. When I got to Declan's boat, the numbers were impressive, even by Pototanga standards. "It seems that Declan and his anglers—Henry and Eloise Standard, from Massachusetts in the United States—landed thirty-two salmon today, including several bright fish. Let's hear it for the Standards," I said, clapping my hands until the other guests and guides joined. (The feat was that much greater considering that Henry had only one arm. He had figured out a way to cast by anchoring the butt of the rod against his thigh, and used his left foot—and sometimes his mouth—to reel the fish in.) Declan was smirking as I described the Standards' day. "Do you have something to add, Declan?" I asked.

"In fact I do," he began, standing. "You might say that the Standards caught thirty-three fish today. As one fish was caught twice. You see, we were just slamming the fish down in the Ledges. It was good *craic*." He rolled out "craic" with an exaggerated brogue; he's a born entertainer. "After lunch, Eloise cast out and hooked a beautiful buck salmon, bright as a shilling. Now the Ledges is called the Ledges because it is punctuated with a number of—yes, ledges. The fish shot downstream at a perilous rate, and then bolted left, as if it knew that the sharpest of the ledges resided there. Perhaps it did."

Declan paused to take a slug of his lager, then continued. "Eloise had at least fifty yards of line out, so her backing was no doubt sawing back and forth across the rocks. Sure enough, poof! The line goes limp, and the fish is gone. Fortunately, Eloise was fishing a running line that was well taken care of. I always tell our anglers, *clean. Your. Lines.* Though the fish was no longer connected, Eloise's running line was high in the water column, floating slowly downstream with the current. I figured that at least we could get her kit back, so I hauled up the anchor and we floated down. When we reached the running line, I noticed that while the end attached to the severed backing was floating downstream, the section attached to the shooting head and the fly were moving slowly upstream, meaning—the fish might still be on. I grabbed the running line and the severed end of Eloise's backing and tied a quick nail knot, praying the fish would stay still. It did. When the knot was completed, I asked Eloise to reel in. Within three cranks of the reel, she was tight to the fish a second time! On this occasion it ran upstream, steering clear of the aforementioned ledges. It was a long fight, but we got him to the net." With that, Declan made a small bow, and sat down.

Perhaps the Ledges would one day be renamed "Twice Caught."

CHAPTER THIRTY

Tunnel of Sámi Love

ELYSE WAS IN A CONTEMPLATIVE MOOD AS WE SPED DOWN-stream toward the Z'ablee beat. I pointed out a Steller's sea eagle. She smiled, glanced up and returned to her electronic pad. I slowed the boat down to point out some Sámi petroglyphs on a rock wall below Double Fantasy. She smiled, glanced over and returned to her electronic pad. She knew to dress warmer than on our previous boat ride, so the snuggle that I hoped would be reprised was not forthcoming. I must have sighed audibly—*quite* audibly to be heard over the engine's roar—for Elyse felt the need to close her pad and address me.

"I am not unhappy with you, Cody, nor indifferent to the sur-roundings. But this is a solemn time. A man's life may be in the balance. This *cojones*." I choked back at a giggle at her brief lapse into slightly profane Spanish. "I am brushing up on my knowl-edge of Sámi. So I can be of usefulness if needed." I appreciated her small malapropisms as I enjoyed Dmitry's. But it was obvious that a metaphoric Sámi was blocking this ride through my tunnel of love.

I had reason for concern myself. Had I negotiated tense situ-ations in the past? I certainly had:

PROBLEM: Two unacquainted anglers are sharing a boat on the Blue River. The first angler refuses to pinch the barb down on his stonefly nymph as it might make him "lose his one shot at a trophy," and proceeds to embed his fly in the cheek of the second angler. The second angler, bleeding profusely and screaming like a banshee, grabs an aluminum rod case with the intention of striking the first angler.

SOLUTION: I grab the rod case from the second angler before he can deliver a blow to the first angler's head and tell the second angler to sit still and please be quiet. I position the hook residing in the second angler's cheek so the barb is exposed, clip off the barb with my Leatherman tool, slide the offending nymph from the impacted cheek, apply first aid cream and a small bandage, and inform the first angler that, henceforth, all flies fished in my boat will be barbless so we don't have any more situations like this.

PROBLEM: On the Deschutes River fishing for steelhead with a friend who used to play collegiate football. We hike forty minutes in the dark to fish a favorite run. A guide with two clients slides his boat in a hundred yards below us at first light, with the intention of "low-holing" us. My collegiate football friend (who played on the defensive line) wants to walk down and drown the offending guide.

SOLUTION: I calm my collegiate football friend down and tell him I'll take care of the situation. I walk down to the boat, where the two sports are standing and stringing up their rods, and tell the guide I want to talk to him. He steps out. I remind him of the etiquette of steelheading, that low-holing is a breach of said etiquette, and he should move on to a different run, as we were there first. He replies that it's a free country and he'll fish his clients wherever he "goddamn wants." I explain that my friend upstream is 6'6" and weighs

280 pounds and would be happy to walk down and speak to the guide if I flash my headlamp three times. The guide steps into the boat, tells his sports to sit down, pulls anchor and rows to the other side of the river.

Yet neither of these—with the possible exception of the low-holing incident on the Deschutes—had life-or-death consequences. I thought back to my discussion with JD many months before concerning why he thought I'd be a good candidate for the position of camp host at the Pototanga. He'd said "equanimity." Calmness. Composure. Evenness of temper in difficult situations. If I could remain myself, would I be able to rectify the situation? I couldn't help but imagine the precarious scenarios Quinones might be tangled in:

- Strapped to a stake in the river with only his head exposed above the water
- Laid out on a rock with each limb attached to a reindeer, drawing/quartering imminent (and probably quite painful, as reindeer would not likely pull as hard as stallions)
- Shackled in a small enclosure where there was barely enough room for air to pass through, thus denying him any opportunity for athletic expression

Rounding the horseshoe bend above the wide expanse of Z'ablee, we came upon quite a different scene. Igor and several Sámi accomplices—two of whom were young and hardy, more resembling members of the band Led Zeppelin in their heyday than the old man on the cover of *Led Zeppelin IV*—stood by the river's edge, waving. Behind them was a simple corral holding a number of reindeer. There, several other Sámi were looking on and applauding as Quinones completed a headstand on top of one post before launching into a back flip. I cut the engine and drifted to shore, where Igor's friends waded in to grab the boat's prow and pull us to the bank. They extended a hand to Elyse, which she accepted with a smile. I dropped the anchor and hopped out.

"The young man Cody by the river," Igor said, coming to shake my hand. As the hand he extended was that of a kidnapper and potential killer, I wasn't eager to take it, but instinct and custom kicked in and I shook it, perhaps a bit too vigorously. "*Bures!*" I replied, showcasing my limited mastery of the Sámi language.

"Hello Cody," Quinones called over from the corral. "Thank you for rescuing me. And hello Elyse!" Elyse curtsied in response.

One of the other Sámi men presented a platter with some small cubes upon it—reindeer cheese (*renost*), I presumed. I smiled and shook my head, though Elyse sampled one and said "*Buorre.*" It was not hard to imagine that a bottle of some sort of Sámi moonshine might come out next, made of—fermented reindeer milk? And the thought of a little picnic on this bright summer day above the Arctic Circle, in the company of Elyse, was not unattractive. But this was a hostage negotiation, not a day in the park. Though Quinones was not playing the role of your typical hostage.

"I suppose we should discuss the situation here," I said to Igor, nodding toward Quinones, who was now attempting a headstand on the gunwales of my boat. "Perhaps Elyse could act as our interpreter." She smiled and curtsied again. "You have taken Quinones as a"—prisoner didn't seem quite the right word, so I backtracked—"You have taken Quinones. We would like him to come back to our fishing camp." Elyse nodded and then slowly translated. Igor nodded and then replied in a sing-song voice that was quite calming, given the situation. Elyse furrowed her brow for a moment, then translated back.

"The reindeer like to swim. Your friend wants to swim with them."

I must have looked perplexed, as Elyse tried again. "The reindeer like to swim. You want your friend, let them swim."

"They like to swim?" I repeated. Igor must have read my expression; no translation needed. He signaled to a few of his men by the corral, who turned back some barbed wire that served as a gate. A large male specimen trotted out, and the other reindeer—a dozen or so—followed him toward the river. They were not shy about entering the water, stepping in one right after the other. I expected them to cross quickly to the other side, but they reached the deepest spot in the run and began swimming slowly in a broad circle, heads tossed back with a slight grimace, a sign, perhaps, of reindeer joy. Not surprisingly, Quinones soon dove into the river and joined the reindeer daisy chain, alternating between a breast, butterfly, and backstroke. Igor looked on proudly, then spoke at length. Elyse prepared to translate again.

"Cody, this is not word for word, but it's close," she began. "Igor says that the act of swimming is essential for the reindeer's well-being. It is exercise, it is stress relief. It improves the quality of their milk and their meat. It is a source of happiness. And this is their favorite swimming spot." Igor helped himself to a cube of cheese and continued. Elyse followed suit. "The boats make the reindeer scared. Vroom! Vroom! They won't swim. They won't make milk."

"Please tell Igor that the Pototanga Lodge is willing to forego its privilege to bring anglers to fish the waters of the Z'ablee beat," I replied. "Given this act of good faith, we would ask that you release the Pototanga Lodge's general manager, Emanuel Quinones, into our custody." Elyse wrinkled her nose and tilted her head, a gesture that suggested I could do better. I tried again. "Please tell Igor that we won't fish here any more."

"That's more like it," she said, and then relayed my message. Igor nodded, but his face remained stern. Then I remembered Dmitry's coda. "Please tell Igor that Dmitry will send you his thumb if this is not true." Once Igor heard this, his withered features melted into a smile, and a bottle was produced.

Should the promise not be kept, I imagined that it would not be difficult for a man of Dmitry's station to produce a proxy right thumb. And it would be quite difficult for Igor to verify the hypothetical thumb's provenance. But as Quinones rejoined us on the bank, it didn't seem to matter. We passed around the bottle and shook hands. The spirit—which *was* fermented reindeer milk—was no worse than the Brennevin some Icelandic guests had brought to the lodge earlier in the season. We said our goodbyes and I pointed the jetboat back up river.

The ride upstream was longer and bumpier then the trip down to Z'ablee. Quinones soon curled up in a ball and fell asleep near the prow, tuckered out from his cold swim and a few slugs of the Sámi liqueur. Elyse sat in the seat toward the back, leaning against me occasionally as waves from a passing rapid jolted her in my direction. Fighting the current in our upstream advance, I found myself overcome with feeling for her. Her calm and decorum during the translation sessions with Igor. Her good nature. Her pixie haircut and tiny nose ring and rosebud mouth. Motoring into Double Happiness, I kneeled down so our faces were even. I touched her cheek with my hand ever so lightly. When she didn't flinch, I closed my eyes and pressed my lips against hers. She didn't push me away.

The Tunnel of Love I'd so dreamed of had come to pass, in at least a small way.

CHAPTER THIRTY-ONE

There Is a Season . . .

ELYSE FLEW BACK TO MURMANSK AND ON TO HELSINKI ON THE Saturday following Quinones's rescue. Though a day of her research was lost during the Z'ablee incident, she was still able to compile all of the information necessary to provide a blueprint for the Pototanga's transition to solar power, and collect enough data to produce a feasibility study for greening up the lodge's septic system. She also found the time to accompany me on a leisurely walk to the Illipanga, to the little clearing where I'd first met Igor and his reindeer more than a month before. I'd brought the makings of a little picnic, including one of the better bottles of red wine that Quinones kept hidden away in the office for VIP guests. There was a consistent breeze with a hint of the cooler weather that would soon arrive, enough to keep the bugs at bay. We walked side by side at first; when the call of a cuckoo startled us and she grabbed my arm, we began to hold hands. At the clearing, I laid out a little blanket. As I was fumbling with the corkscrew and the Burgundy I'd liberated, Elyse set her hand on mine and shook her head. Then she lifted off her pink sweater and gently pushed me down.

And then she . . .

And then I . . .

And then we . . .

And thus we began what I hoped would be a long-term exercise in *experiential research.*

The summer doldrums that had descended upon the Pototanga in early July seemed to depart with Elyse. Cooler temperatures reduced the bug populations to more manageable levels, and waves of fresh fall-run fish began to arrive upriver, making THE HOME POOL worth fishing again. Full-freight paying customers soon followed; their general prowess and tipping potential energized the guide corps and elevated their spirits . . . though the latter could have been as much the anticipation of deliverance from the Pototanga back to places with roads, night clubs, and fast food (even Murmansk had a Subway and a Burger King). Some of these "whales" (as the guides referred to the well-heeled guests that reserved their fishing for late August and early September, our most expensive weeks) were less than personable; a few downright officious. But a handful seemed to understand that in addition to any hard work and intelligence they'd exercised, their good fortune was the happy result of a cosmic crapshoot—being in the right place at the right time, knowing the right people, having the right skin pigment and a name without too many (or with enough) vowels. They seemed to recognize that those of us working at the lodge, the little people at the ticket counters and flying the planes and helicopters were humans much like them, with aspirations, families, and passions of their own.

Quinones spent more and more time away from the lodge that last month of the season. This might have been a response to my handling of his "abduction" (and a heightened level of confidence in my leadership skills), though it was more likely a result of the enthusiasm Igor's younger colleagues showed for parkour; Quinones had willing acolytes and was ever eager to share his wisdom. But he made sure to be present, along with a number of his new Sámi friends, at the Pototanga's end-of-year party.

It was a lodge tradition to throw a great celebration the last Friday of the official season, after the last paying clients had reeled in their Willie Gunns and Ally Shrimps, broken down their Sages and Loops, and tucked their Hardys and Bogdans away in their shearling-lined cases. For many of the Pototanga's behind-the-scenes staff—the kitchen workers, the handymen, the mechanics—it was the year's great coming-out event, a chance to interact with guests and let their hair down. More than a few chose to dress in costume for the event, and long-time guests joined in the fun, carrying alter egos to the lodge in their finely hand-tooled leather luggage along with their angling kit.

It had been difficult to assess JD's day-to-day contributions during the month he'd spent at the lodge, beyond a significant depletion of our lager and red wine stores. But on the days preceding the party, he became a whirlwind of activity, stringing colored lights along the interior walls of the dining hut, calligraphing personalized invitations for each lodge guest and employee, and building a large papier-mâché pinata in the shape of a salmon, filled with plastic airline bottles of vodka and cognac; the stick for hitting the pinata took the form of a miniature spey rod and was also lovingly crafted by JD in the Pototanga's wood shop. If there was one thing that JD understood, it was how to throw a good party.

And quite a party it was. The normal plated sit-down dinner was abandoned in favor of a buffet featuring the remnants of the Pototanga larder—everything from snow crab and reindeer fillets to halibut cheeks, Chicken Kiev, and, confusingly, bánh mì sandwiches. The last of the lager kegs had been tapped, and half-consumed vodka bottles seemed to occupy every surface. An elaborate sound system had been installed and was pumping a playlist alternating between Norwegian death metal, Russian hip-hop, and the occasional balalaika ballad, perhaps from Dmitry's friend Pyotr. As the evening wore on, the costumed dancers—some dressed as politicians and long-dead kings, some as characters from *Star Wars* or *Game of Thrones*—were no longer dancing as much as swaying together in a slow, rugby-like scrum. At one point Dmitry attempted to call in to wish the partygoers well, but it was impossible for him to be heard over the tumult, and he hung up after thanking me for making sure nothing burned down.

When it was time to break the piñata, few were in any shape to be swinging a stick of any sort. Several guests swung and missed and fell down in the process. One of the Sámi guests, not quite comprehending the conventions of piñata breaking, grabbed the salmon and held off those who approached him with the little spey rod. As he backed out of the dining room with his prize, he tripped and fell on the piñata, which easily cracked under his weight. The little bottles of liquor spilled forth, and the revelers spilled outside, as most of the spirits in the dining room had by that time been consumed.

I refrained from drinking that evening, as it seemed like *someone* should remain sober should a life-threatening situation present itself. Though no small number of brain cells perished, guests and workers steered clear of the river, the heavy machinery, and any sharp edges of furniture. It was no doubt a somber helicopter ride back to Murmansk the next morning, the din of the Mi-8's engines matching the static of revelers' hangovers. I rose early to make sure there was at least coffee for our guests, and to collect the festivities' debris. I was joined by Roman, our pastry chef, who favored dark tinted glasses at all times of day. He had also abstained the previous evening, on religious grounds. "Why do the Russians drink so much?" I asked as we collected broken vodka bottles.

"We are a traumatized and melancholy people," he said, sweeping up broken glass. "It suits us. Though technically, I'm from Ukraine."

Another abstemious onlooker that evening was Geoffrey Simms, a "whale" who hailed from New Canaan, Connecticut. He looked on at the party with a level of detachment, yet not in a judgmental manner; he seemed genuinely curious about the drunken goings-on. And equally curious about what had brought someone like myself to a remote fishing lodge above the Arctic Circle. I told him a bit about my time at university in Montana and the years I'd spent—perhaps misspent—on the Blue. He confided that he'd pursued a number of different vocations before landing in the publishing field, and that while time might seem wasted through a short-term lens, all of one's experiences, good and bad, influenced who we become. As managing director of an international publishing conglomerate, he believed his work as a barista, advertising copywriter, security guard, ski instructor, and insurance adjuster had all proven useful. "It's all about grasping the human condition," he concluded. "And having understanding and empathy for what people want and need—two different things." Before retiring to his cabin, he handed me a business card. "I think you might find the publishing field of interest, Cody. Managing a lodge is not unlike managing an imprint. Corralling individuals from many different disciplines and pointing them toward a common goal. With a light touch. I hope you'll call me."

I assured him that I would. But that it would probably be in the spring.

Before the celebration had launched in earnest, Quinones had called me to his cabin. "As you may know, Dmitry and the Pototanga Lodge have a sister operation of sorts at the tip of the South American continent," he said, while doing chin ups on a bar he'd installed in his doorway. "Tierra del Fuego. The land *of fire*." He paused at the top of a chin up for dramatic effect. "The general manager for that property—a very good woman—has been called to serve in the National Congress of Argentina. This has created a vacuum. And nature abhors a vacuum, as does Dmitry." He dropped to the floor and began a vigorous set of one-armed push-ups. "Dmitry believes that you could fill that vacuum, given your performance this summer. Your quarry—the sea-run brown trout, is a close relative of the Atlantic salmon. Your clientele—many of the same faces that grace the guest list of the Pototanga." He flipped over and began a series of crunches.

"I should add that your friend Elyse will be on the premises for several weeks this January to conduct a green audit of *that* facility. And that as you'll be the general manager—the *head cheese*, as you Americans say—your compensation for the season will be commensurately greater."

"What about JD?" I asked, the memory of his pre-party industriousness still front of mind.

"Mr. Smithers will be staying in Russia for the immediate future. He will be working with Dmitry on some *special* projects," he replied, his eyebrows raising dramatically. "I also understand that Mr. Smithers is to be *married* to a *Russian* bride." This was the first I'd heard of either development. But JD never shared his intimacies with me, and he was a man ever shrouded in mystery and surprises.

I told Quinones I would definitely consider his offer, though in my mind I had already accepted. The notion of Tierra del Fuego certainly held a romantic appeal, made no less romantic by the promise of Elyse's visit. And of course, there would be time between the end of our season and the beginning of the season on the Rio Grande to permit a visit to Baker, a few days of swinging flies for steelhead . . . and, of course, a stopover en route in Paris (which Elyse and I had already mapped out over numerous Skype calls).

Once the last guests were carried north, the staff spent an additional week preparing the lodge for a long Arctic winter. It was basically a reversal of all the preparations of the spring, though conducted with a bit less vigor; after all, no guest arrivals were imminent. On the afternoon before the staff would begin their departure, Roman and I were securing some of the food-stuffs that could survive the winter—flour, lard, sugar, and such—in a solid steel container outside of the kitchen that resembled a safe. Though we never encountered bears during the season, one large specimen had laid the kitchen to waste some years before after a stick of butter had been left behind; the brown bear's sense of smell is said to be seven times that of a bloodhound. JD, who'd been spending most of his waking hours fishing THE HOME POOL, stuck his head in.

"Cody, can I have a word?"

I excused myself from Roman and joined JD in the dining hall, where the tables, the lights, and the bar had been packed away. A few aluminum folding chairs remained, and we took a seat. He produced a few cans of Sierra Nevada pale ale from his jacket. We popped the tops and toasted.

"It's been quite a voyage, Cody," JD said. "Less than a year ago, you were a fishing guide. A fishing guide, I'd say, who was . . .

"Lacking direction," I suggested.

"Rudderless is more like it," JD continued. "A good guide, but rudderless. A guide's life is okay for some. Good fun. A chance to perhaps connect emotionally with a few of your sports. But I saw something in you that could do more. That wanted more. Could reach more people in a positive way, while also burnishing your own patina, as it were. So I plucked you from what one might call relative obscurity and placed you in a position where you could shine."

While I didn't care much for his choice of words, I couldn't argue with the logic.

"And shine you did, my young friend," he continued, clapping me on the shoulder. "Like a bright, shining star. You steadied this at times listing ship. You liberated a man from danger. And you even found a little action on the side," he concluded with a lascivious wink. "I imagine many big things lie ahead," he added, raising his can in another toast.

I was certain he knew about Dmitry's offer of the Rio Grande and perhaps even the line of communication with Mr. Simms. He'd once said he had eyes and ears everywhere on the river. Perhaps on *every* river.

"What lies ahead for you, JD?" I asked, hoping to shift the attention away from me.

"As Quinones may have mentioned, I will be remaining for an undetermined period in the Russian Federation, both to attend to several discrete assignations that Dmitry has asked me to resolve, and of course, to celebrate my pending nuptials with one Svetlana Vasiliev, whom you will know as Svetlana, the Pototanga's lead server. As fate would have it, we'd already become acquainted and courted, in a matter of speaking, on the World Wide Web. Imagine my surprise to arrive here and find her at my beck and call!" On cue, Svetlana poked her head into the dining hall, procuring two more cans of Sierra Nevada from her apron, and departing with a deep bow. "I'm a lucky man." We popped open the cans and toasted once again.

"We would of course be honored to have you in attendance, but understand that you will be otherwise occupied, quite literally at the other end of the world. But rest assured that a hiatus at Doña Maria Lodge will be part of our around-the-world honeymoon extravaganza. Perhaps you will lead Svetlana to her first sea-run brown."

Roman appeared in the doorway. "I think we can lock her down," he said, referencing the food protection box, though he could just as well have been speaking to the entire Pototanga operation. I excused myself from the tent, as I held the keys.

ACKNOWLEDGMENTS

This book would not have been possible without my many angling friends, and their good humor and willingness to share many stories from their experience. These include Geoff Roach, Mac McKeever, Peter Gyerko, Ken Matsumoto, Joe Runyon, Mark Harrison, Tim Purvis, Kenton Quist, Mike Marcus, Nelson Mathews, Tom Botkin, David Moscowitz, Hamp Byerly, Rob Crouch, Chris Conaty, Ken Helm, Frank Groundwater, Paul Ainslie, Peter Marra, Mark Tegen, Dinty and Ali Leach, Allen Sing, Phil Sgamma, Dave Welty, Robert Tomes, Steve Cook, Greg Thomas, Conway Bowman, and Kirk Deeter. I've enjoyed many days on the river with these friends, and treasure them all as my angling and health become harder to mend. May our many shared water memories be an inspiration, even a blessing, for you all, and inspire future aquatic adventures with those you hold dear.

I appreciate the fine editors I've had the good fortune to work with; in addition to some of the folks above, this would include Nick Roberts, Mike Floyd, Steve Duda, Tom Bie, and Geoff Mueller.

I also extend a deep bow to my bandmates Sloan Morris, Keith Carlson, and Doug Mateer, who've helped put fly fishing to music in our band, Catch & Release. Thanks go to several early readers of the manuscript, including Doug Levin, Virginia Miller, and Dave Tegeler. I also wish to acknowledge the creative efforts of Keith Carlson, Sarah Mahoney-Voccola, and Tim Romano, who helped bring the book into being . . . and Max Phelps,

Judith Schnell, and Justine Connelly at Globe Pequot/Lyons, who believed in the project. Finally, I want to extend a special thanks to my family, who've humored my absence on far too many occasions so I could pursue my favorite pastime . . . my wife Deirdre, daughters Cassidy Rose and Annabel Blossom, and Lola, who rescued us, and has accompanied us on many waters. And to my parents, Tina and Andy, who were not anglers, but always encouraged me to pursue my passions.

POTOTANGA LODGE